"You're Penelope Lear," Tucker said. **"Who doesn't know the Lears of Anchorage?"**

"That isn't who I am."

"You aren't Penelope?" He stayed close to the fire, watching her gather herself. Lamplight flickered, casting shadows on a face that was beautiful in a way he wouldn't have imagined. Maybe because of the light in her eyes, the animation of her features.

"I am Penelope Lear. But…but I'm not a spoiled little rich girl." In the warm glow of the lamp he saw tears pool in her blue eyes.

"I'm sure they'll be looking for you."

"Of course they will." She shivered again.

But would they find her?

Alaskan Bride Rush:
Women are flocking to the Land of the
Midnight Sun with marriage on their minds

W9-AVR-166

Books by Brenda Minton

Love Inspired

Trusting Him
His Little Cowgirl
A Cowboy's Heart
The Cowboy Next Door
Rekindled Hearts
Blessings of the Season
   "The Christmas Letter"
Jenna's Cowboy Hero
The Cowboy's Courtship
The Cowboy's Sweetheart
Thanksgiving Groom

BRENDA MINTON

started creating stories to entertain herself during hour-long rides on the school bus. In high school she wrote romance novels to entertain her friends. The dream grew and so did her aspirations to become an author. She started with notebooks, handwritten manuscripts and characters that refused to go away until their stories were told. Eventually she put away the pen and paper and got down to business with the computer. The journey took a few years, with some encouragement and rejection along the way—as well as a lot of stubbornness on her part. In 2006 her dream to write for the Steeple Hill Love Inspired line came true. Brenda lives in the rural Ozarks with her husband, three kids and an abundance of cats and dogs. She enjoys a chaotic life that she wouldn't trade for anything—except, on occasion, a beach house in Texas. You can stop by and visit at her website, www.brendaminton.net.

Thanksgiving Groom
Brenda Minton

Steeple
Hill®

Published by Steeple Hill Books™

If you purchased this book without a cover you should be aware that this book is stolen property. It was reported as "unsold and destroyed" to the publisher, and neither the author nor the publisher has received any payment for this "stripped book."

Special thanks and acknowledgment to Brenda Minton for her contribution to the Alaskan Bride Rush miniseries.

STEEPLE HILL BOOKS

Steeple
Hill®

Recycling programs
for this product may
not exist in your area.

ISBN-13: 978-0-373-81510-4

THANKSGIVING GROOM

Copyright © 2010 by Harlequin Books S.A.

All rights reserved. Except for use in any review, the reproduction or utilization of this work in whole or in part in any form by any electronic, mechanical or other means, now known or hereafter invented, including xerography, photocopying and recording, or in any information storage or retrieval system, is forbidden without the written permission of the editorial office, Steeple Hill Books, 233 Broadway, New York, NY 10279 U.S.A.

This is a work of fiction. Names, characters, places and incidents are either the product of the author's imagination or are used fictitiously, and any resemblance to actual persons, living or dead, business establishments, events or locales is entirely coincidental.

This edition published by arrangement with Steeple Hill Books.

® and TM are trademarks of Steeple Hill Books, used under license. Trademarks indicated with ® are registered in the United States Patent and Trademark Office, the Canadian Trade Marks Office and in other countries.

www.SteepleHill.com

Printed in U.S.A.

But they that wait upon the Lord shall renew their strength; they shall mount up with wings as eagles; they shall run, and not be weary; and they shall walk, and not faint.

—*Isaiah* 40:31

This book is dedicated to Doug, for being my hero each and every day. And to my kids for chipping in and making it so much easier.

Chapter One

Lost in the Alaskan wilderness.

Penelope Lear's great adventure was not supposed to end this way, with her standing on a shadowy path in the middle of nowhere. Mountains surrounded her, cutting her off from the rest of the world. She was completely, utterly alone in a world so huge she didn't know in which direction to turn.

What had started with her brilliant idea that she could find the treasure and save the town of Treasure Creek was now looking like a news alert. All because she was positive she'd seen a clue from the treasure map. Just days ago when she'd taken a hiking tour of the area, she really thought she'd seen the rock formation that people were talking about. Her dad would have told her she was less than a week in town and already in over her head.

Instead of the confidence she had started out with, she was picturing the headlines that would be splashed across newspapers tomorrow morning. Or whenever they finally realized she was missing.

"Penelope Lear, Heiress, Lost in the Alaskan Wilderness."

She didn't want to think of other headlines, worse headlines. But she couldn't stop herself from thinking about what would happen if someone didn't find her. If they didn't find the Jeep and her note that she was hiking out, heading south toward Treasure Creek, what would happen?

As for heading south, she hoped she was heading south.

She glanced at her watch and then looked west, where the sun would have been setting in an hour, if not for the mountains encircling her. At least she *thought* she was looking west. She had a compass in her bag, but she didn't know how to use a compass. It had been part of the equipment she'd bought at the general store.

The clerk had grinned at her when she'd bought supplies. Either because he was single and enjoyed all the single women trotting through Treasure Creek and his store, or because he thought she was another clueless city slicker.

Fortunately Joleen Jones had bounced into the general store in time to take some of the pressure off. Joleen with the hair, the clothes and the personality to draw attention the way sugar drew ants. Joleen, like so many other women, had come to Treasure Creek looking for the hunky tour guides described in the *Now Woman* magazine article.

In the short amount of time Penelope had been in Treasure Creek, she had realized she wasn't the only woman who had shown up to see what the men of Treasure Creek were all about; if they really were different.

Penelope insisted on being married to the man of her choosing, rather than the man with the right business portfolio.

Cold seeped into her bones, pulling her back to the present and her horrendous situation. Penelope pulled her coat a little closer and took a few careful steps on the trail.

November in the Alaskan wilderness. She'd lived in Anchorage her entire life. Even if she had spent her time in the city, she should know something about the Alaskan wilderness, something more than the fact that it was cold. And dark.

Yeah, she should know something—like stay home where it was safe and warm.

She hitched her backpack over her shoulder. At least she had jerky to eat, a few bottles of water and a rain poncho. And matches. If it came down to it, she could build a fire.

A noise, just a rustle or maybe rocks shifting under someone's careful steps, caught her attention. She froze, and then turned cautiously, carefully. Chills were sweeping up and down her spine, tingling through her scalp and arms. She didn't want to be dinner for a bear. Or a mountain lion.

How far back had she left the Jeep? It had to be miles. She'd been walking for hours. Not that going back would do her any good. Something had run out in front of the vehicle a few hours ago and she'd veered, sending the blasted thing over a small ledge and into a ditch. It wasn't going anywhere anytime soon.

If only she hadn't allowed herself to get distracted. But instead of paying attention to the trail that passed for a road, she'd been daydreaming about the Chilkoot Pass, an icy trail over the mountains that had claimed many lives back in the late 1800s as settlers hurried to Alaska, hoping to find gold. Instead they'd found greedy traders, icy trails and death.

She'd been imagining that trail, with steps cut into the ice. She'd been imagining how her ancestors might have felt as they walked into this frozen land, and how it might have changed their lives. She had imagined wagons and livestock left behind.

She hadn't imagined crashing a rented Jeep or getting lost.

She pulled her cell phone out of her pocket and she lifted it, hoping for a signal and still not getting one. So what was her story going to be, since "lost because of her imagination" didn't work?

Maybe people would believe her if she said Bigfoot ran across the trail in front of the Jeep? She shivered again, imagining Bigfoot. Of course that was just a story. Bigfoot wasn't real. She was sure he wasn't. More than likely. She peeked around again, just to make sure she wasn't being followed.

The November wind whipped through the pass, straight through her coat. She wasn't one of those settlers looking for gold in the Yukon, looking to make her fortune. She was a Lear, daughter of Herman Lear, one of the wealthiest men in Alaska. Or maybe *the* wealthiest man in Alaska. She didn't need gold.

She needed a map.

She knew how to read a map. She knew

more than anyone had ever given her credit for. She wasn't arm candy or an empty-headed socialite.

That thought brought back leftover anger and her brother's words when he'd heard her plan. He had told her he didn't believe she could survive a day in the small town of Treasure Creek, let alone in the wilds of Alaska. But she had insisted she could. She didn't need fancy boutiques. She didn't need pedicures.

At the moment she needed help. She yelled again, hoping she'd hear more than her own voice echoing back.

Good gravy, Miss Mavy, what a mess. But surely someone would come looking for her. Amy James, the owner of the Alaska Treasure's Tour Company. Or that police chief; if he wasn't too busy trying to keep people from stealing maps. If he wasn't too busy looking for Tucker Lawson—the last person to go missing in the Alaskan wilderness. Someone would realize she didn't come back to the Inn. Maybe the receptionist who had invited her to church when she first showed up in town. It had amazed her how easy it was to get to know people in a small town. Until someone rescued her, she'd do her best to get herself out of this mess. And then, when they found her, the headlines would be about the heiress who survived the wilds of Alaska, not the heiress who got lost.

And eaten by bears.

She shivered and started walking again. The trail she was on seemed to go south. Or she assumed she was heading south. With mountains towering around her, how was she supposed to know?

She'd stay on the trail heading "south" and she'd pray.

And she wouldn't get distracted. She wouldn't stop to look at trees that reminded her of the Treasure Creek treasure map that Amy's boys had found by accident several months ago.

She picked her way along the trail that grew narrower as she walked. And it didn't look like the path most taken. It looked like a forgotten trail to nowhere.

She was surrounded by high peaks, towering pines and shadows. A branch cracked somewhere in the brush to her left. Penelope stopped, frozen to the spot. She held her breath and waited.

What if Bigfoot was real, not a legend?

A mountain goat crashed through the brush and hit the trail twenty feet ahead of her. Now she knew who had made this trail. And it wasn't a guide or hikers.

She kept walking, keeping her gaze on the trail, listening to the rush of a stream bouncing off rocks. Something crunched under her foot. She glanced down at the white stick and shivered. What if it had been the poor, lost lawyer, Tucker Lawson?

He'd disappeared months ago. She'd heard all about him when she'd eaten dinner at Lizbet's Diner. She had loved sitting with the crowds that gathered there. She loved pretending to be a part of the community, a part of their group of friends. They had shared stories with her about the town, about the treasure they hoped to find, and the struggles they'd seen of late. She'd learned that Amy's husband had died suddenly a few months ago, leaving the town and Amy in mourning. She'd also heard how Tucker Lawson had come home to see his dying father but hadn't made it in time. Tucker had been flying his small plane when it crashed somewhere in the wilderness.

According to the folks at the diner, the one good thing that had happened was an article about the town that had been meant to bring in tourists and instead it had focused on Treasure Creek's hunky bachelors bringing swarms of single women to the tiny town of seven hundred.

Penelope had listened, thankful that they hadn't known who she was, because had they known they wouldn't have shared. But Penelope's heart had been touched by their plight and by the desire of the community to keep their little town strong.

And she knew that she could help. Her family and small circle of friends thought that she was really only good for spa days and charity functions, but that's because they didn't understand her heart and how much she really wanted to help others.

No one had ever really understood her. Obviously her dad understood her less than anyone, or he wouldn't have taken it upon himself to find her a husband, to insist that it was time for her to settle down.

Treasure Creek had given her a chance to be the person she always wanted to be.

Penelope stopped to brush stray tears from her cheeks. It was getting cold and she'd have to find shelter soon. And she could do that. She'd watched those survivor guys on TV. She had matches. She had food, water and a rain poncho. Little children survived in the mountains, surely she could, too.

She could even fish. She'd done that on the

guided tour she'd taken a couple days after getting to Treasure Creek. Oh, but one little problem: no fishing pole this time.

A shadow flashed on the ground in front of her. She looked up, shading her eyes with her hand. The bald eagle swooped and circled before landing in a tree. Penelope closed her eyes and remembered the painting on the wall of her room at the bed-and-breakfast in Treasure Creek. She recalled every single detail with vivid clarity.

A painting of a bald eagle, and the words "They that wait upon the Lord shall renew their strength, they shall mount up on wings as eagles. They shall run and not grow weary, they shall walk and not faint," from The Book of Isaiah.

Wait on the Lord. She could do that. She was new at faith, but she could wait.

Faith, that was her real reason for coming to Treasure Creek. Oh sure, there was the added bonus that she might find a real man and not get stuck with the man her father had picked. She didn't even know the man, but she knew the type. He'd be motivated and serious—and all about his career. And she'd be left at home, wishing someone cared.

That wasn't going to be her life. Not anymore.

She was going to find someone who would really love her, and who wouldn't want to change her.

The plan had formed just a couple of weeks ago, when she'd been at the day spa getting a manicure and facial. As she'd waited for her toenails to dry, she picked up an old issue of *Now Woman* magazine and read the article about the hunky men of Treasure Creek and the lack of available women. There had been pictures, and Penelope made a decision to get herself one of those men.

But she had noticed something else in the article. There was a paragraph about the town, about their faith in God and the belief that He would get them through their hard times.

The words had hit Penelope in the heart, where she'd felt empty for as long as she could remember. She'd spent her life trying to help others, to be more than just Penelope Lear, socialite.

And no one had noticed.

So she'd packed her bags and headed for Treasure Creek in search of the life she wanted.

She wouldn't have any life at all if she didn't keep walking and find a place to make a shelter. With sticks and her rain poncho. She could do that.

A snarl behind her stopped Penelope in her tracks. She froze, too afraid to even turn and face what was behind her. It stepped on twigs and leaves, crunching, probably close. She could stay and get eaten, or run.

She turned to get a closer look and her foot slipped. The bear opened its mouth and roared. She grabbed at a tree, reaching for a limb. Her fingers grasped, and then slipped. She continued to slide, slipping down the steep sides of the ravine. She screamed, and screamed again.

Tucker Lawson had left the lodge hoping to bring home meat for himself and the Johnsons. The missionaries were a nice couple, and since their garden had been providing food since he showed up at the abandoned lodge during the summer, he had been the one to provide meat. Usually fish.

He walked along the trail, enjoying the quiet, breathing in the fresh air, and feeling... almost peaceful.

The guilt was still there, though, a double load of it. How did a man get past not speaking to his father for years, and then getting home too late, getting home just in time to bury his dad, but not in time to say goodbye?

He shifted the gun he carried and stopped,

looking out at the quiet afternoon, shadowed and gray. The mountains loomed, blotting the sunshine that might peek through the clouds this time of year. Possible, but not a great possibility. But being close to the coast, at least they weren't buried in snow. For November, that was a plus.

It was just cold. And soon it would be dark. And he didn't want to be out here in the dark. The wilderness was huge and it could overwhelm a guy, make him feel almost claustrophobic because it closed in around him, keeping him in a cocoon that was safe but confining.

Sometimes he thought about going back to civilization, back to Seattle, back to his law practice. But when he considered his return, he felt the weight again, heavier.

So he stayed in the mountains with the Johnsons, missionaries who had served God their entire lives but were now questioning, searching and trying to find their own way back to sanity and to faith.

God... Tucker felt so far from God at that point, he couldn't begin to think about faith. He could look out at a creation that astounded him with its beauty, and he could see the hand of God. He could feel only devastation.

Tucker never had the chance to tell his dad that he loved him.

He moved on, taking the trail carefully because it had a tendency shift, move to other locations. It was made by animals, and it followed their paths.

As he walked, something crashed in the woods behind him. He turned, raising the gun. A mountain goat jumped across the trail and ran off into the thick woods. Tucker lowered his weapon and walked on. He wasn't in the mood for hunting.

They could have potato soup again. Or canned beans. He didn't really care. The walk was better than hunting. Out here, away from everything and everybody, he could clear his mind. He could think.

Something screamed. He stood for a moment, waiting for it to scream again. The big cats sometimes sounded like a screaming woman.

But they didn't typically follow the scream with "Get out of here, bear."

And then she screamed again.

A woman? In the middle of nowhere? How in the world had a woman gotten out here?

She screamed again and he ran down the trail, waiting for her to scream again so he could pinpoint her exact location. And then he saw her at the bottom of a small ravine, sitting on her backside, waving a stick at the bear that stood on hind legs a few feet away.

Strands of her long blond hair tangled around her face. She scrambled back, crab crawling and then managing to get to her feet.

Alone? How in the world had she gotten out here? By his estimations, they were a good fifteen or twenty miles from Treasure Creek.

He shot into the air, then he slid down the ravine, down to where she was standing. The bear lumbered off in the other direction. Tucker grabbed her, throwing her over his shoulder.

As he hurried up the nearest trail, she was still screeching, bouncing against his back. Her words came out in garbled squawks. "Put…me…*down*."

He wished he could.

"If you don't stop fighting me, and stop screaming, I'm going to leave you here."

"Fine, leave me here. I can take care of myself."

"Of course you can."

He glanced back over her shoulder. The bear had lost interest, but that didn't mean they were in the clear. He shook his head at seeing a bear this time of year. Shouldn't the thing be hibernating? He kept walking, kept hold of her legs as he scrambled up the hillside.

She was blubbering about the bear and how it was going to eat her. He nearly laughed.

"It was just a cub. It wasn't really going to eat you."

They reached the top of the hill. He stopped, gasping for one deep breath of air, and then he deposited her on the ground.

Great, that's what he needed. Not just any female, but a crazy one. A crazy female with eyes the color of the sky and blond hair tangling around the face of a Norwegian princess. She stood in front of him, tears streaming down her cheeks, twigs tangled in her hair

In that moment, he recognized her. Not a Norwegian princess. Worse—the daughter of Herman Lear. That was exactly what he didn't need. Especially if she'd gone crazy out here.

"It wasn't a cub. It was huge. And I looked like its dinner." She wiped at her eyes and then gasped as she took a step.

"What's wrong?"

"I think I twisted my ankle on my way down that hill." She peered up at him, eyes narrowing as she studied his face. "I'm fine."

They took another step and Tucker couldn't take it anymore. He scooped her up in his arms, ignoring the way she fought against him.

"I can take care of myself."

"Oh, that's pretty obvious." Did he need to explain that she was in the middle of nowhere and had just happened upon the only bear not hibernating? Obviously taking care of herself wasn't her strongest trait.

"Do you think he'll chase us down?" She glanced over his shoulder, back in the direction of the ravine. "Bears do attack people. And eat them, I think."

Tucker shook his head and resisted the urge to laugh. "You think that bear would eat you?"

"He might have. And now how am I going to find the trail out of here? I'm sure I was going in the right direction. If I'd stayed on that trail—"

"Do you think you could be quiet? I really wouldn't want to come into contact with the mother of that bear cub."

"It wasn't a cub," she whispered. "Besides that, you have a gun."

It was over his other shoulder, pointing at the sky. It was a reminder of why he'd come out here today. He'd been hunting for food, not for silly heiresses.

And what was he coming home with? The heiress.

"Are you Tucker Lawson?" She kept talking, and his regrets kept growing. It was probably too late to take her back to the ravine.

"Back to that silence clause in our rescue agreement." He shifted her weight in his arms and she grabbed at his shoulders.

"I don't think I agreed to silence. I'm just asking if you're Tucker Lawson."

"Yes, I'm Tucker Lawson." He glanced down at her, and then glued his eyes back on the trail and the long walk ahead of them.

"They're looking for you."

"What does that mean?" Of course he'd been gone awhile, but he'd mentioned when he bought supplies, before he'd started out, that he planned on being gone a good long while. He'd told his office to give his cases to his partner.

"You disappeared, and a lot of people are worried."

"I didn't realize."

Another ten minutes of this and he was sure he'd want to give her back to the bear.

"They've been searching for you. Especially your friends, Jake and Gage."

"How are they?" It wasn't as if he'd been out here all these months without thinking about his friend, or what everyone back in Treasure Creek thought about his disappearance.

"I've only been in town about a week, but from what I've seen, they're doing really great. Worrying about you hasn't stopped them from falling in love."

"Falling in what?"

"Don't make it sound like they fell in a pile of something nasty. They've fallen in love. Millions of people do so every day."

"In love with whom?"

"Well, I don't know Jake that well, or Casey…"

"Don't tell me he's dating Casey Donner."

"I think it's more like engaged and planning a wedding. There's talk around town that he's waiting to find you, wanting you to be his best man."

"What else has happened?"

"Romance, I guess. Dr. Havens and his nurse. I really believe Joleen and Harry Peters will get married. Won't that be a sight, to have Joleen stay in Treasure Creek?" She rambled on and he didn't have a clue what she was talking about. He kept going back to the idea of his childhood friends in love. "Anyway, they're all really worried about you."

He'd tuned out her chatter and missed most of what she said until she got to the last part, about people worrying about him. It wasn't as if he hadn't thought of that, that people would be searching. He'd just hoped they found the note and realized he was safe.

"As you can see, I'm fine. If I wasn't, you would still be back there with that bear cub."

"The bear wasn't a cub." Penelope knew when to change the subject. She looked up, studying his face—the sandy brown hair that was a little on the long side, and hazel eyes that glinted with flecks of gold. He didn't look like this in the pictures they put up in town. Those were pictures of a lawyer lost in the woods. In the photos plastered in the paper and all over town, he was slick, with short hair, expensive suits and a cynical expression. The type of man her father would have on his team.

The type of man her father would probably love to have for a son-in-law. The type of man she detested.

Instead of being the man on the poster, Tucker Lawson was capable and strong. He looked like most of the men in Treasure Creek, dressed in jeans and a heavy jacket. He was broad shouldered and rugged. He was so handsome he made her mouth water a little. The way it watered when she looked at a yummy dessert.

"He was this year's cub." His words were clipped, short. "You could have run at him and he would have been scared to death." He huffed as he walked. "Why don't you tell me what you're doing out here, miles from town?"

"Hiking. What else?"

"Alone?"

The word *alone* bounced around inside her mind.

She glanced away from him, at the looming shadows as dark fell. She had been about to stay the night in the Alaskan wilderness, alone. And now she was in the arms of a stranger who had saved her from a bear. She really felt like crying.

What kind of man stayed out here, though? How in shock had she been that she hadn't immediately thought about that, about him and how unsafe she was at that moment in his arms?

"I had problems with my Jeep." She blinked furiously. "I can walk. I shouldn't really go any farther. Someone will come looking for me."

He grunted and kept walking.

"Listen, I can take care of myself."

"I think you've proven that point."

"My backpack. My stuff. I need my cell phone."

"Honey, you don't need your cell phone, not out here. Who are you going to call, Smokey the Bear?"

"It might work. There might be a signal they can follow."

"Who, Smokey the Bear?"

"Rangers, police, people who rescue other people."

"They'll follow you to a ravine in the middle of nowhere. Now please, stop talking."

"I can't." She started to shake—uncontrollable shaking—and her breath came in short gulps. "Please, just let me go."

A million thoughts whirled through her mind. She was miles from anywhere. She was alone with a man who had disappeared into the woods. She had walked hours after ditching the Jeep. No one would know where to look for her. She didn't even know if she was going south. She struggled, thinking if she could get away. If she could get down and run.

He stopped walking and peered down at her and then he shook his head. His arms tightened around her trembling body. "I'm not going to hurt you."

"Right, of course you're not." She wanted to stop holding his shoulders, but she couldn't convince her hands to cooperate. She needed to wipe away the tears. Common sense told her to be brave, to show him he couldn't hurt her. "I know karate."

He laughed. "That's great to know. You could have used it on the bear."

"You think I'm joking. I took a class in self-defense."

"I believe you. But you won't need to use it on me. I'm taking you to a nice safe place and a sweet older couple who will look after you."

"There are other people out here?"

"There are." He started to walk again and her body was still trembling. Shock, fear and cold were sinking into her bones. "Calm down, we'll be there in a few minutes."

She nodded, but her eyes were blurring and her vision became a pinpoint. She wanted to be strong. She wanted to fight him. Instead the world faded. She heard him telling her to breathe. She was sure she was breathing. She could feel her heart pounding hard. And then nothing.

Chapter Two

Tucker took large steps in the direction of the old lodge he'd called home for the past few months. It was his own fault she'd passed out. He should have told her about the Johnsons sooner. He should have seen the panic in her face, noticed the second when she realized how alone she was. He jostled her a little, but she didn't wake up. This was just what he needed.

Or didn't need.

The lodge appeared—a dark, shadowy place, hidden in the mountains. Unused for over twenty years, it didn't have electricity and they were using an old pump for water. This place was his haven.

And now he had to share it with a screeching, high-maintenance female. He continued up the path. She was getting heavier. She wouldn't thank him for mentioning that.

He carried her up the steps, then had to maneuver to get the storm door open. The inside door opened as he pulled the storm door. Mrs. Johnson pushed it all the way open for him to get inside. Her eyes widened when she saw the woman in his arms.

"Where did you find her?"

"In the woods."

"Is she okay?" Mrs. Johnson followed him down the hall to the small parlor they used most often now that it was cold. It was easy to close off, easy to heat.

"She's fine. She got herself worked up and then she passed out cold. A little exhaustion, a lot of fear."

"Who is she?"

"My guess, Herman Lear's daughter, Penelope."

"Oh, my. Are you sure?" Mrs. Johnson pulled a throw blanket off the couch and he took the hint and placed the woman on the worn seat of a sofa that they'd had to beat the dust out of just a few months earlier. The Johnsons had been here about a month before he showed up.

"Yes, I'm sure." He'd seen her pictures. He

knew her father. She was Penelope Lear. And she was the last person he wanted to see.

"Goodness." Wilma Johnson clucked, the way she'd clucked over him more than once.

"Wake up." He patted Penelope's cheek as Mrs. Johnson stood next to him, leaning in, watching. "Ms. Lear, time to wake up."

She blinked and looked at him. "Where am I?"

"A hunting lodge."

"People live out here?" she murmured.

"People do. It isn't necessarily the most inhabited part of Alaska, or the most civilized, but here we are."

She scrambled to sit up. Mrs. Johnson patted her shoulder. "There, there, sweetie, you're safe. And don't worry about Tucker, he's lacking social skills. We'll take good care of you until we can get you back to safety."

"Thank you, Mrs....?"

"I'm Wilma Johnson. My husband and I were staying here. And then Tucker came along to stay with us."

Penelope looked back at him. "They think you're dead."

"I'm obviously not. But why would they think that?"

"They found your plane, blood and then no sign of you. They haven't given up, though."

Tucker sat down in the chair near the fire. He needed a minute to soak in the idea that the folks in Treasure Creek assumed he was dead. He hadn't considered that. He should have, though. Wilma was busy untangling Penelope's hair, pulling small sticks and leaves from the blond strands. The older woman shot him a look, her lips pursed.

She was a mother at heart. She had lost her only child, but that didn't stop her from mothering. She'd been hovering over him for months, trying to fix him, to fix his heart. And it had been a long time since anyone had mothered him.

"I'm going to make tea." Wilma stepped away from Penelope and he knew what she was doing. She was leaving them to share their stories.

He watched her leave the room and then he turned, facing the woman who had sat up, but still held the blanket tight around herself. He got up to put wood on the fire.

"I was on my way to a friend's cabin." He shoved a log into the fireplace, poking it into place with the metal poker and then standing back as sparks shot up and flames licked at the mossy bark. "The plane stalled out on me and I landed on that lake. I did hit my head as I came down, but I managed to get out and to walk here." He had walked for three days, he explained, and he'd been as lost as he'd ever been in his life.

"I know they've searched a large area around the lake."

"I hadn't meant to cause panic. I even left a note on a tree, that I'd find shelter and that I was on my way to a friend's cabin. Not that I made it to that cabin. Mr. Johnson found me wandering the woods. Concussion I guess. I don't know how far I walked from the plane. And you, Ms. Lear, what brought you to Treasure Creek? Are you hunting for a rugged outdoorsman? A man to share your life and your heart with, as that infamous article stated?"

She glared at him and he wanted to smile. "How did you know my name?"

"You're Penelope Lear. Who doesn't know the Lears of Anchorage."

"That isn't who I am."

"You aren't Penelope?" He stayed close to the fire, watching her gather herself. Lamplight flickered, casting shadows on a face that was beautiful in a way he wouldn't have imagined. Maybe because of the light in her eyes, the animation of her features.

"I am Penelope Lear. But, but I'm not a spoiled little rich girl." In the warm glow of the lamp, he saw tears pool in her blue eyes.

"I'm sure they'll be looking for you."

"Of course they will." She shivered again.

But would they find her? Penelope huddled into the blanket, glad for its warmth, and for the fire. Her ankle throbbed and her throat was dry and sore. Probably from screaming at the bear.

"I have to try to get out of here, back to Treasure Creek. I have a compass in my pocket and I know I need to go straight south."

"Straight south from where?"

Okay, that was a fair question. "From where I left the Jeep."

This was not the way to prove her intelligence. She cringed a little as she replayed her words.

He smiled a little. At least he didn't laugh at her. "Do you know where you left it? What direction you went? Where you got lost?"

"No." The truth—stark, kind of cold and not what she wanted to admit to. "No, I don't have any clue. I left the Jeep and started in the direction I thought was south. I guess that was about seven hours ago now."

"You've never heard you're supposed to stay in one place if you get lost?"

She glanced away from him. "Of course, but does anyone follow that rule?"

He hadn't. "No, but they should. And I'm

afraid that means you're stuck with us for a little while."

She flipped the blanket back and stood, wobbling a little as her weight settled on her swollen ankle. She bit back an exclamation and he watched her, as if he wasn't sure what she'd do next.

"I can't be stuck here. I have to—"

Brows arched. "Have to what?"

She sank back onto the couch, because it was no use. She had to find a husband who would love her. Cynical eyes didn't want to hear about love, about a father who thought he could pick the perfect mate for his daughter.

It sounded positively Victorian when she said it out loud. Her friends had laughed when they heard.

"Nothing." Why should she care if she got stuck here for a year? Maybe this was God's plan, for her to hide here. And perhaps her father would forget his plans.

Tucker Lawson pushed himself up from the chair. He sat down on the edge of the massive coffee table and reached for her foot. She flinched but bit back her protest as he lifted it.

"If we had ice, we'd ice it down." He touched the darkened flesh and she squeezed her eyes closed. "Bad?"

"Not at all." She opened her eyes and he was watching her. Cynicism had been replaced by concern. He held her foot, hands gentle but rough and calloused. Not the hands of a lawyer, she thought.

No, he had the hands of a man who had been living off the land for several months. A man with broad shoulders cloaked in a flannel shirt. She remembered that he smelled of soap, not cologne or aftershave. He smelled of the outdoor air and laundry detergent.

He reached for a pillow and placed it on the table. As he stood he propped her foot on the pillow, easing it down gently. She stared at him, not sure what to do or what to stay.

"Thank you for rescuing me."

"You're welcome." His voice was gruff, dismissive.

She wanted to tell him she wasn't a bad person. She wasn't another empty-headed socialite, intent on fun and not caring about others. She wished she could tell him she hadn't traveled to Treasure Creek thinking she might find a husband. That would have been a lie. What woman didn't want to find her dream man?

She thought it started for most girls when they turned five and had their first kindergarten crush. It was downhill from there. Every boy—and then man—that looked at them had the possibility of being "the one" they would marry.

She could have told him he had nothing to worry about. That would have been the truth. He was definitely not her type. He was the type her father wanted for her. He was a successful lawyer with connections and enough money that Herman Lear wouldn't have to worry that he was after the Lear fortune.

For once she kept her mouth shut. She didn't want Tucker Lawson to know how she felt about her life, or how much she wanted a new one.

She was reinventing Penelope Lear. That was no one's business but her own.

"I'll see if we have anything in the first aid kit." Tucker stood in the doorway, his face in shadows.

"Okay." She answered, still lost in her thoughts about her life and what she would have wanted it to be.

And he left her alone in a room lit with just a lantern, candles on the mantel and the firelight.

Tucker knew he should take her back to Treasure Creek at first light. If she could have walked, it would have been doable. But with her injury, they couldn't walk it in a day.

They'd have to give her ankle time to heal. And then he'd have to take her back to civilization. He'd have to go as well. And he wasn't ready. He didn't know if he would ever be ready to go back.

To have it be Penelope Lear who forced him back, that made him a little itchy around the collar.

Just this past May, Tucker had said a polite "no thank you" to that offer. He had heard that Herman Lear had approached several other men, most of whom lived in Anchorage and were well connected. One of them had probably taken the offer, and that had sent her running to Treasure Creek.

A little bit of pity scolded him for being too harsh with her. No one should be married off that way, as if she were a stolen painting up for bid on the black market. There was no dignity in that kind of bartering.

He lifted the candle he'd taken from the parlor and walked down the dark hall in the direction of the kitchen. She was probably hungry as well as thirsty. From the aromas drifting down the hall, a combination of wood smoke and soup, he thought that Wilma Johnson had thought the same thing.

The kitchen was lit with lanterns and candles. Mr. Johnson, Clark was his first name, sat at the small table, a cup of coffee in his hand. He looked up from the book he was reading and smiled at Tucker.

"Found a stray?"

Tucker nodded. "Yeah, I guess I did. Her ankle is swollen and bruised. I don't think it's broken."

"I have an Ace Bandage and we still have pain relievers." Wilma dished soup into a bowl. "I hope she doesn't mind something as simple as vegetable soup."

"She'd better not." Tucker grabbed the first aid kit. "She'd best be grateful."

"She's been nothing but polite, Tucker." Wilma Johnson patted his arm. "I'll take her the soup and tea. You have something to eat. It might take the snarl out of you some."

He had to smile. "Yeah, it might. More soup, Clark?"

Clark Johnson shook his head. "I'm done. You go ahead and eat. She did a bang-up job on it."

Tucker dished out a bowl of soup and poured himself a glass of water from the pitcher on the counter. He took both and sat down across from Clark. "I guess you know who she is?"

"That I do." Clark looked up from his book, lantern light flickering between the two of them. "We'll have to find a way to get her back to Treasure Creek. They'll be looking for her. And besides that, a young woman like Penelope Lear can't make it out here, living the way we've been living."

"How do you propose we get her back to town?"

"You'll have to take her." It was said matter-of-factly, as if it would be easy to go back.

"I'm not ready to go back."

"Neither are we. But she's another case. She didn't ask to be here, to be in the wilderness."

"No, she didn't. They'll send search teams. I'm sure her father will have the army out if he can manage it."

"They've probably searched for you, too. They haven't found you yet."

"I didn't want to be found." Because it was easier this way, hiding from people, from his pain.

Or at least he told himself he was hiding.

Tucker ate his soup, preferring to let the conversation end the way it had, with him ignoring the obvious. She would have to go back to town. She couldn't stay here with them. And as much as he didn't want it, too, it would affect him.

When he walked back down the hall, he heard her soft voice, telling Mrs. Johnson how she'd gotten lost, about the bear, about him rescuing her. He could imagine her eyes wide, full of excitement as she reinvented the story, making it more amazing than it had been.

The bear hadn't been a grizzly. It hadn't been huge. It wouldn't have eaten her.

He walked into the room. It was dark, lit with lanterns, a few candles and the fireplace. Penelope Lear sat on the worn sofa and Wilma sat in the chair nearby.

Penelope looked up, the bowl of soup held in her hands. She smiled at him and managed to look like this was normal to her—being lost in the woods, staying in a house without electricity or running water. He'd seen her home, albeit from a distance. This was anything but normal.

Wilma tossed him the Ace Bandage. He caught it, looked at it and wasn't at all sure what she wanted him to do.

"I don't have a clue how to do that." Wilma smiled sweetly.

"It just has to be tight." He wanted to toss it back. He didn't want to touch the foot of an heiress. He didn't want to deal with someone who spent her time working on a tan rather than working at life.

In her defense, she wasn't tan. Her skin was a natural creamy color, with just the barest hint of gold. She was staring at him, waiting for him to move or to say something. He'd never been at a loss for words, not once in his life.

That was his reason for becoming a lawyer. He knew how to argue, how to drive a point home. He knew how to make his case and to persuade people to understand his side of the argument.

He'd argued himself right out of his father's life.

"Tucker?" Wilma Johnson had stood. She was holding Penelope's empty bowl.

He shook himself from the past and looked at the long cloth bandage in his hand. In the dim light from the lantern and the warm glow of the fireplace, Penelope waited. Wilma had walked out of the room.

He pulled the chair up close and reached for her foot. She grimaced a little but didn't complain.

"It has to be tight." He explained. "Sorry, I'm not a doctor. My only experience with Ace Bandages is from high school basketball."

"That's more experience than I have."

He wrapped the elastic bandage around her foot and ankle. It was more swollen, more purple than before. "We're going to have to keep you off it, I think. Do you have a problem sleeping in this room? It'll be warmer and the Johnsons are just down the hall."

"I'm fine with that." She looked up, blue eyes dark in the shadowy room. "What about you?"

"I'm a big boy and I'm not afraid."

"I mean, where do you sleep?"

"Upstairs."

"Oh." She let out a breath and looked pretty relieved.

"There you go. It's still early. I'll light another lantern, and if you'd like, I can bring you a book."

"I'd love a shower." She glowed rosy pink and looked down, at the cup of tea she still held.

He wanted to laugh, but couldn't. He'd traumatized her enough for one day. Instead he did his best "hoping to make you feel better about your situation" voice. "I'm afraid a shower is out."

"Out?" She looked up. He imagined that most people would have built a shower for her if she'd looked at them like that.

"No electricity, no hot water. No running water, actually."

"Oh."

"I take it you hadn't meant to rough it quite this much."

She shrugged, "I hadn't thought about it. But actually, I did want to rough it, Mr. Lawson. I came here to prove…"

She didn't finish. That had him more than a little curious. It had been a long time since he'd been curious. He sat back down, ready to hear what she wanted to prove.

"Prove what?"

"Nothing." She lifted her cup and sipped, ignoring his questioning looks. But he wasn't about to give up.

"Oh come on, Penelope, we're both here for reasons that the rest of the world can't understand."

She lowered the cup. Teeth bit into her bottom lip and she studied his face. Her eyes overflowed again. "I'm sorry about your dad."

He drew in a breath, amazed that five words could change everything. He'd been playing with her, teasing. And she had laid him low with a soft look and words of compassion.

What did he say? Did he tell her she couldn't begin to imagine how this felt? He didn't know her well enough. He thought he might get up and walk out. But he couldn't leave her sitting on the sofa in this lonely room.

"Thank you," he finally answered, the only words that he could say. He could no longer question why she was here. He thought maybe she had good reasons.

Maybe she was escaping a father who thought he could control her life. From what he knew of Mr. Lear, that was more than plausible.

"I can't get you a shower, but tomorrow Mrs. Johnson can help you heat water for a bath." He stood and really wished that Wilma would reappear. He wasn't a nursemaid or a nanny. "I can get you a book to read."

"A book would be good."

He would bring her a book, and then he would escape to his room. Not what he normally did at six in the evening, but tonight he wouldn't mind being alone. More than anything, he wanted to be as far from Penelope Lear as possible, because she had brought his old life into this safe place. She had reminded him of everything he'd been running from. And she was exactly the kind of woman he didn't want to deal with.

"Tucker, thank you."

He nodded as he walked out the door.

Chapter Three

Penelope woke to a steady chopping sound. She sat up, brushing hair back from her face and blinking a few times to clear her vision. The room was in shadows. That didn't mean it was early, it meant it was winter.

She glanced at her watch. It was almost nine. Her second day lost in the wilderness. Her second day in these clothes. Not much she could do about that. She left her one change of clothes in the ravine with her backpack.

The most pressing matter was to find a cup of coffee. If they had coffee. She stood, flinching a little when weight hit her foot. But it wasn't as bad as she thought it would be. She took a few careful steps. And then she saw it: sitting on the chair by the door was her backpack.

Tucker had gone back for it. She picked

it up, opened it and sorted through the one change of clothes, her cell phone—worthless that it was—and the bottle of water.

The door opened and Wilma peeked in. "Well, you're up and around. Would you like coffee and breakfast?"

"I'd love coffee and breakfast." She'd love a shower, a toothbrush and toothpaste.

"Come on down. Can you make it okay?" Wilma looked at her foot, shaking her head. She was a sweet lady, with dark hair and eyes that were so kind, Penelope wanted to know her better and maybe keep her in her life for a long time.

"I think so. It doesn't feel that bad today."

"Good. And later you can change clothes and we'll wash the ones you have on."

"Without running water?"

Wilma smiled and laughed a little. "We'll heat water and wash them in a tub. And you can take a bath, too."

"That would be wonderful." She set her pack back on the chair. "How did it get here?"

"Tucker went out early, hunting, and he brought it back."

"Hunting?"

"Yes, hunting. He didn't get anything,

though. I think sometimes he uses hunting as an excuse to walk."

Penelope peeked through the opening in the curtains. The chopping sound again echoing in the quiet morning. She saw Tucker swinging an axe at a log. Of course, they would need firewood. He swung again, connecting, splitting the log. As if he knew she was watching, he glanced toward the house. He couldn't see her though. He swiped his arm across his brow and continued to chop.

Wilma smiled and started down the wood-paneled hall, in what must have been the direction of the kitchen and the most wonderful aromas.

"How do you cook?" Penelope followed her.

"Wood burning stove in the kitchen."

Of course, that explained the smokey smell. They walked into the kitchen. A lantern hung from the ceiling, and dim light came in through the windows. No curtains. The room was walled with pine paneling and the floors were stone. It was warm, and the sweet smell of something wonderful and baked scented the air.

"I made muffins. It isn't easy in that old stove, but they turned out decent." Wilma placed two muffins on a plate. "Pour yourself a cup of coffee and have a seat."

The coffee pot was on the stove, an old blue pot like the ones she'd seen in antique stores. Penelope took the cup that Wilma handed her and poured the dark liquid into it.

"Would you like me to pour you a cup?" She turned to Wilma, who had set their plates on the table.

"Oh, no, I've had plenty. My heart races if I drink too much coffee."

Penelope carried her cup back to the table and sat down, wincing a little. Her ankle throbbed from the short walk down the hall. Wilma watched her, brown eyes warm, full of compassion.

"Not better today, is it?"

"I thought it might be. I was hoping. Thinking if it was, I could head toward Treasure Creek."

"You can't do that." Wilma shook her head. "It's too far."

"But they'll be worried. My family will be worried."

"They'll search for you. Maybe they'll find you here. If not, you're going to have to wait until you can walk. It isn't a short trip to Treasure Creek from here."

"How did *you* get here?"

"We flew in. A friend has a helicopter and he put us down in a clearing a short distance away. He drops supplies occasionally. We do have a map, and we can find our way out if we need to, but it isn't a short walk. It certainly isn't one you can make with a sprained ankle."

Penelope bit into the muffin, glad that it was sweet and still warm. She needed a minute to get herself together, to stop thinking of this as a disaster that would only prove to her father that she needed a keeper.

She could survive out here. Even if it meant chopping wood and hunting for her own food. Even if it meant using the old outhouse she'd been introduced to last night. She could make it in the wilderness because she had survived in worse places. And when she got back to town, she would help Amy find the treasure.

She did wonder why the Johnsons had felt a need to hide away in this cabin, far from civilization.

"Does the cabin belong to your friend?" Penelope wiped her fingers on a napkin and fought the urge to reach for another muffin.

"It belongs to his uncle. Years ago they used it for hunting. They would bring out groups and rough it for a week. The uncle got sick and the cabin sat here empty, other than an occasional relative coming out for a few days to get away from it all."

"It is definitely 'away from it all.'" Penelope would have liked to share with Wilma Johnson that this wasn't her first trip that landed her far from civilization. It wasn't even close to being the most difficult place she'd ever stayed in.

Tucker headed down the trail, searching for more signs like the ones he'd seen earlier that morning. Penelope had been with them all of forty-eight hours and already she was bringing trouble their way. He wasn't going to say anything to her, but he definitely wasn't going to let her out of the house alone. Not that he'd have a lot of luck keeping her inside. Wilma had found an old wooden crutch in the attic.

They'd had company during the night. And it hadn't been the kind of company that knocked on the door. It had been the kind that sneaked around in the gloom, leaving boot prints in the snow and breaking branches off bushes as they pushed around in the dark. They were too far from civilization for that kind of company.

For now, he'd keep his discovery between

himself and Clark Johnson. But it proved his point that Penelope Lear was trouble.

"Hey, where you going?" A singsong voice called from behind him.

Great, just what he needed. He considered going on, pretending he hadn't heard. From what he knew of her, she'd just pick up speed and track him down. But she'd also probably find some way to get into trouble in the process. He stopped walking and turned around.

There she was, his punishment for all the wrong things he'd ever done. She hobbled after him, smiling brightly. A stocking cap was pushed down on her head, framing her face. Every now and then the crutch under her arm tangled with roots or got caught on rocks. She'd hobble, nearly fall, and then right herself.

It didn't help matters that she was carrying a fishing pole in the other hand. Great. He didn't have to guess what she was up to today. Yesterday she'd nearly smoked them out of the house in her attempt at fire-building in the fireplace. Today she was going to fish.

Peace and quiet. That's what he'd found out here until he'd dragged her out of the ravine two days ago. One moment, one second of weakness, and all of that peace and quiet was gone. Sucked out of the world. By this one female.

If he could walk her out of here today, he would. It would save them all a lot of trouble. But if he took her out, it meant he'd be returning to the real world.

He wasn't ready to give up his time here.

But how long could a guy stay lost in the wilderness, locked away from reality? He knew that this couldn't last forever. Even the Johnsons knew that eventually they'd have to return to civilization. They'd all have to make some decisions about their futures.

They discussed it last night, after Penelope had fallen to sleep. The Johnsons had talked about their son. He'd spoken about his dad. He still wasn't talking about the devastating news he'd gotten from Seattle before he left Treasure Creek.

He was still processing that. He was still trying to figure out how he had become this person, a man who no longer knew where he came from or where he was going.

"What are you doing out here?" He waited until she was nearly next to him. "In those boots, and with a fishing pole?"

The boots were ridiculous things, mostly fur and no real sole. He shook his head and then looked up, meeting blue eyes that flashed with humor.

She smiled, and the gesture nearly knocked him on his back. When she smiled like that, a guy needed to be warned. That smile could change everything a person thought about her.

"Give a man a fish and he'll eat for a day…" she recited.

"Teach him to fish and he'll eat for life." He shook his head. And then he got it and he didn't feel like smiling. "I'm not teaching you to fish."

She didn't pout, but the laughter in her eyes dissolved and she just stared at him. "But I thought we needed something for dinner."

He looked at her, at the pole, and he shook his head. Clark should teach her to fish. That would be better. And then there was the ankle situation.

"It's a little bit of a walk to the stream."

She shook the crutch at him. "Did you forget what Wilma found in the upstairs closet."

"Wilma's very handy to have around." There had to be other reasons he could think of for not taking her. "It's rough going."

"I can handle it."

He was losing. "Why are you so determined to do this?"

"Because." She shrugged slightly. "Because I have to do something. Because I'm not helpless."

"You're not running from someone or something?" He tried to make it sound like a teasing question, but it wasn't. He wouldn't let her put the Johnsons in danger if she was hiding something.

"No, I'm not running from anything." But she looked away, as if maybe she was.

"Really? I don't know if I'm going to believe that."

She glared at him, her nose flaring a little. "I'm not running. I'm—"

"What?" He smiled. "Did you come to Treasure Creek looking for a husband? Let me guess—you read the article in *Now Woman,* and since you're a little bored with your life, you came to Treasure Creek to find an adventure and one of those single, hunky tour guides." No way was he going to feel jealous over that. No way.

"I came because of people like you."

"What does that mean? I'm pretty sure you didn't come here looking for someone like me."

"I came to get away from people like you. You think you know me so well, and you don't. You think I'm nothing more than

Herman Lear's daughter. You think I shop, get my nails done and party."

"And I'm wrong?"

"I don't have to explain myself to you. I came to Treasure Creek because I wanted to know what it was like to be somewhere—" she looked away "—somewhere like Treasure Creek. And really, since you're not willing to tell me everything about you, why should I have to tell you everything about me?"

"I just asked what you were running from." He spoke in a softer voice, because the softness in her tone pushed him back a notch. Not only that, but he wasn't getting any answers by pushing.

"I'm not running from anything."

He stared at her for a moment before nodding. "Come on, then. But I'm warning you, be quiet. If you jabber nonstop, I'm using you for bait."

She hobbled closer to him, smiling again. "Thank you." Right. He took the pole from her hand.

As they headed out, he glanced around them, making sure they weren't being followed. He tried to tell himself that the footprint in the damp ground had been his imagination. Maybe it had been *his* boots or Clark's that had made the imprints in the muddy ground. It didn't have to mean that someone was watching them.

But if someone was, it wasn't about him, or the Johnsons. They hadn't seen a sign of anyone in months. He glanced sideways at the woman next to him. She was tall, her expression was serious but animated. She was definitely determined. And if they were being watched, it had something to do with her.

Penelope walked next to Tucker. Tiptoe-ing on her left foot to keep the weight off her ankle. He walked slower than she knew he would have liked—for her. She smiled a little.

He wasn't what she'd come to Treasure Creek looking for. He was too much like what she'd left behind. She could see it in his eyes, that he was driven, that he was all about his career. She had spent her life with men like Tucker. Her father was one. Her brother was another.

And the women in their lives were forgotten trophies. Their wives, girlfriends and daughters were paraded when needed. They were dressed in designer gowns, draped in jewels and taken out on the town when an event required their presence. And then they sat at home, or entertained themselves when the men lives were busy with their careers.

She was positive that not everyone in their circle of friends lived that way. She had friends from college who had gone on to pursue careers. Her mother had friends in business. It was just the life of a Lear. Or a Lear woman.

But not today, with Tucker Lawson walking next to her. They were going fishing. She smiled again, because this was her adventure. This was Penelope Lear reinvented.

She glanced at Tucker in his faded jeans, hiking boots and the heavy jacket over his flannel shirt. She could imagine him in a suit, standing in a courtroom or sitting behind a massive desk. She wasn't the only one reinventing herself.

They continued on in silence, walking on a trail that was rocky and sloped downhill. Trees were sparse here, leading down to the stream. Back at the cabin they were heavy and towered toward the sky.

The rushing water of the stream could be heard before the stream came into view. But when she saw it, she had to stop, had to stare. Clear water rushed, pounding over rocks and boulders. Downstream, just a short distance, the swift moving water slowed and pooled.

"Wow."

"Yeah." Tucker held her elbow and

guided her over the rough terrain. "You're stubborn."

"So I've been told. And people always manage to make it seem like a bad thing. But it could be good, if you think about it."

He smiled and shook his head. "Sure. Of course."

"Wilma sent lunch with me."

"Did she really?" He led her to a place at the edge of the stream where animals had stopped to drink. Hoof and paw prints were still visible in the soft earth. Something had dug near the edge of the water.

Penelope studied the paw prints. "What made these?"

He shrugged. "Everything. Elk, bear, fox. Up here, so far from any kind of settlement or town, there is just about anything you could imagine."

"Do you think we'll catch fish for dinner?"

He handed her the pole. "We can try."

"What do I do?"

He laughed. "Cast your line into the water."

"You say 'cast' like I should know what that is."

He moved behind her, his arms wrapping around her. He took the fishing pole in his hands and guided hers. "Cast it easy. Don't throw it out there. Just a nice, easy swing, and then you have to remember to set the hook if you feel a fish bite it."

"Okay, I can do that." She breathed in deep, trying to ignore the way he leaned in close, the way his chin brushed her cheek as he held her, showing her the way to cast out.

She tried, but couldn't ignore the fact that his arms were strong and he smelled like soap and the outdoors. His hands were rough but gentle.

"Of course you can do it." He whispered close to her ear as he helped her cast. "But careful or you'll tangle your line. Don't cast too far or you'll end up with your hook in a tree."

"I can do this," she repeated and swung the rod, watching as the line and the bait flew through the air, and then landed with a soft *plunk* in the calmer pool of water.

"Good job." He chuckled a little. "You know what you're doing, right?"

"No, not at all."

"Then hang in there. You're doing great." He stood back a short distance, arms crossed, and watched her. She glanced back, making quick eye contact before settling her attention on the fishing line.

"Don't stand there like that." She didn't look at him again.

"Why?"

"You look stern and disapproving. Build a fire. Do something."

He laughed, but she caught movement from the corner of her eye and knew that he was doing what she'd asked. And she relaxed, taking in a deep breath. Another glance over her shoulder and she saw that he was gathering wood. Penelope turned back to the water and to fishing. And she smiled, because it was easy to smile out here. Even lost, it was easy to smile.

And then the sudden jerk on the rod. She pulled up on the pole. She could see the gray of the fish. She could feel it tugging, trying to get away. She cranked on the handle of the reel, trying to draw in the fishing line and thus, the fish.

"Tucker!" She glanced over her shoulder. He wasn't there.

She cranked the reel again. The fish pulled, trying to swim away from the hook that had caught it. She took a step backward.

"Tucker. I can't do this."

She glanced over her other shoulder and didn't see him in that direction. She couldn't reel in the fish. She couldn't find Tucker. She yelled his name again and heard crashing in the woods behind her. When she turned, he was there. He took the fishing pole from her hands and pulled it back and then reeled in, pulled it back again and reeled.

"Where were you?" She watched as the fish she had caught came closer to the bank. Fear was replaced by awe. "I caught a fish."

He shook his head. "Yeah, *you* caught a fish."

"What?"

"I think I helped."

She could give him that. "Okay, you helped. *We* caught a fish."

She was responsible for providing food for them to eat. She wanted to dwell on that, but then she remembered that he'd disappeared.

"Where did you go?"

"To look for wood for the fire, remember?"

But there was something in his eyes, something in the way he said it that made her doubt. Firewood didn't crease a man's brow in worry.

And firewood shouldn't cause her own stomach to curl just a little, wondering what he was keeping from her.

But she had caught a fish. She had provided for herself.

Now what?

She shivered a little, not certain if she wanted the answer to that question. What caused the shimmer of fear or danger to crawl up her spine? Tucker? Or whatever it was he wasn't telling her?

Chapter Four

Tucker had never seen anything like it. Standing there in her fuzzy boots and a Shearling coat, Penelope caught three fish. As she pulled in the last one she turned and smiled at him. There was more than a little pride in that smile. And he wasn't about to deflate her.

"That should be enough for tonight, right?" She turned the pole over to him to remove the fish. That, she said, was something she just couldn't do. She had shuddered with her announcement.

"It'll be plenty." He unhooked the fish and attached it to the stringer with the others, then gave her back the pole. "Are you done, then?"

"I'm done. It's getting cold." She looked up at the sky and he did the same.

"Looks like it might snow."

She bit down on her bottom lip and nodded a little. She was a sight, with the pole in one hand and a crutch under her other arm. The wind had turned her cheeks a rosy pink and her nose was red.

"How will we get back to Treasure Creek?" She flicked her gaze away, as if she was looking for a trail out. "I mean, as fun as this is, I really hadn't planned on staying until next spring."

"You maybe should have thought about that before you set out on your own." They headed up the trail, in the direction of the cabin. "Honestly, what were you doing out here, roaming the country by yourself?"

"Are we sharing our secrets?"

"No, I just asked you a question." No wonder her father wanted to marry her off.

She shrugged. "I wanted to find the treasure for Amy, and for Treasure Creek."

He didn't want to laugh at her, but he did. He avoided looking at her, because he knew she'd look hurt by his laughter. He kept the stringer of fish held up and trudged forward.

"You were going to find the treasure? You mean a treasure that has been hidden for generations? A treasure they're not even sure exists? *That* treasure?"

"Stop laughing at me." She stomped ahead

of him with one crutch under her arm, a ridiculous figure in clothes that were suited for the city, not the wilderness. He let her get a little ahead of him because he knew that it would make her feel good, to think she was stomping off, leaving him behind.

And then he took a few steps and caught up with her.

"I'm not laughing at you. But honestly, how did you think you could find it? Do you have the map?"

She pointed to her head. "Up here."

"Oh, of course."

She glared and kept going. "Don't talk to me."

"Okay, tell me how you were going to do it."

She slowed and then stopped, but she didn't turn to look at him. Snow was falling, light flakes floating to the ground on a gray and chilly afternoon. It landed on the crocheted stocking cap that was pulled snug down over her head, and frosted her shoulders.

"I'm so sick of people believing they know me." She turned and a tear streaked its way down her pink cheeks. "You have an image of who you think I am. But do you know that I have photographic memory? If you'd like,

I'll recite the articles I've read about you, and about your disappearance."

"No, thank you." That was a little uncomfortable.

She looked a little smug and he gave her props for not backing down. "I peeked at the map the other day when Amy was showing it to someone. I thought that if I could find the treasure and give it to her, the town would survive. The people of Treasure Creek need that treasure, and I wanted to do that for them."

"You seriously have a photographic memory?"

"I seriously do. I also have a degree in economics."

He opened his mouth—but what did he say to this revelation?

"Shocked speechless?" She smiled and trudged on, that one crutch under her arm, hobbling and hopping every few steps.

"Yes, I suppose I am. And I owe you an apology."

"Because you had me pegged under the stereotypical heading of 'brainless heiress'? Now that we know you're wrong, why don't you tell me about yourself? Did you run from grief, or something else?" She smiled back at him. "A broken heart?"

"I'm not playing this game." Because there

was something sweet and refreshing about her, and he didn't want to ruin it with the nightmares that had plagued him for months. Or the guilt that wouldn't go away. He figured it wouldn't matter. She'd go with the grief and probably make up something about romance gone wrong.

"What about the Johnsons? Why are they out here?"

"The Johnsons have a right to their privacy. Don't play this game with them."

"I'm not playing a game, just asking a question. It's obvious they're hurting. It's obvious that they're kind and good. I wondered what happened to them, that's all."

"And I'm not going to share their story."

"Or your own."

"You got it, Penny."

"Don't call me that."

"Fine. Penelope. Do people in Treasure Creek know who you are?"

She shrugged. "Some do, some don't. It isn't like there's a magazine, *Heiress Quarterly*, or some other ridiculous thing that tells about my life. No, I didn't openly offer my life story to everyone in town. Some knew without me saying a word. A few didn't have a clue and I didn't give them one."

"I see."

"Do you? Do you understand how wonderful it was to eat in a diner and not be recognized? I checked into the Inn and the clerk gave me a room with a view of the building next door. It was wonderful"

"Great." If an heiress wasn't bad enough, make her an heiress wanting to be normal, the type who kicked off the glass slipper and refused to kiss the handsome prince.

The handsome prince thought made him a little uncomfortable because just thinking about her as Cinderella made him envision himself as the prince she might kiss. That had to be proof that it was about time for him to head back for the real world. He was starting to think in terms of fairy tales, and that couldn't be good for a man his age.

So think of something else. He shifted his gaze away from the Shearling coat in front of him and shifted his mind back to the footprints he'd seen.

She kept walking, and he let her get ahead of him. It gave him time to think in silence. It gave him a chance to study their surroundings, to look for anything out of place. Why would anyone want to follow Penelope Lear?

Maybe it was someone who knew what she was worth. Or knew what her father was worth? Maybe someone bent on kidnapping an heiress for a hefty ransom?

If she kept talking, kept getting under his skin, he might turn her over to whoever was after her. No, of course he wouldn't. He wasn't that kind of man. He'd spent last night pacing the floor after having nightmares about a young woman who had lost her life too soon.

He didn't want to have nightmares about Penelope being kidnapped. She might be a thorn in his side and the last woman he wanted to be stuck with out here, but he would keep her safe.

And the less talking they did, the better.

"Why are you walking so slowly?" She paused on the trail and waited for him to catch up.

"Thinking."

She nodded and didn't push. Instead she trudged on in front of him and left him with his thoughts, which now turned to his dad.

They hadn't talked much in the last few years.

His dad should have told him that a bone marrow transplant might save his life. No matter how stubborn the two of them had been, Tucker would have been there for his father. He would have given his marrow and then some to save his dad's life.

It had been the two of them for so long. The two of them against the world, until Tucker had decided to go to Seattle and find his mother. That's when his dad had dug in his heels. He claimed that Tucker had picked money and possessions over family, just like his mother had when she'd run off and left them.

There hadn't been a way to convince the old fisherman otherwise.

Tucker walked next to Penelope and she reached with her free hand to touch his, not holding it just letting her fingers drift over his. He glanced down and she smiled up at him, as if they were old friends.

For a second, a rare second, he considered that.

The moment didn't last, though. If he said a word, she'd have more questions. She'd dig deeper. That's the kind of female she was, the kind who wanted to explore all of the touchy-feely emotions she thought everyone was hiding.

"When we get to the house, I'll clean the fish and you should go sit down and put your foot up."

She nodded a little. "Probably a good idea."

"What? No arguing?"

"No arguing."

She had slowed. He had been so busy thinking about his dad, about the young woman, Anna, he hadn't noticed. Now that he did, he also saw the tight line of pain around her mouth.

But she hadn't complained.

He was having a difficult time shoving her into the box he thought she should fit into. He'd had her pegged as another silly socialite. But maybe there was more to Penelope than he'd given her credit for.

Not that he was interested. He'd had enough of her kind. He figured she'd probably had enough of his. In her world, his kind were a dime a dozen.

Penelope paused at the bottom of the steps that led to the back door and into the kitchen. Her ankle throbbed and her arm was sore from the crutch. She leaned on it and looked up and she didn't want to walk up the three steps that would get her to the door.

"You going to make it?" Tucker held the stringer of fish and her pole. She tried to tell herself this was the lawyer whose picture she'd seen in town. Today he looked like one of the tour guides that had women flocking to Treasure Creek. He was denim, flannel and all male.

"Of course." She managed a smile because she didn't need his help. He had that detached look in his eyes. She knew his kind. He had other things on his mind. He probably didn't realize they were having a conversation.

She knew because she'd seen that look in her father's eyes. All of her life she'd had conversations with men who didn't really listen.

"I'm going inside." She made it up the first step and paused. With her hand on the rail she pushed herself forward, getting to step number two.

"Oh, good grief." From behind her he scooped her up and held her close. "I'll carry you inside, you stubborn female."

Penelope closed her eyes and nodded, not to hide from the pain, but to hide from those eyes of his. Because he looked impatient, but he also looked as if he cared. And he was strong.

He carried her down the hall of the darkened cabin, toward the glowing light of the kitchen and the warmth of the wood stove. She leaned into him, her hands on his shoulders. He had left the fishing pole and stringer of fish, but he smelled of the outdoors.

Wilma Johnson was sitting at the kitchen table. She looked up when they walked through the door. Penelope focused her attention on the older woman, who moved from her chair, pushing another chair out. Tucker sat Penelope down.

"What happened?" Wilma slid another chair out and pointed for Penelope to rest her foot.

"Nothing, just too much walking." Tucker was backing toward the door. "I have fish to clean."

"I'll take care of her for you." Wilma bustled around the kitchen.

"She isn't mine." He walked out the door.

"Such a grouch," Wilma mumbled as she bustled around the room. "I have tea. Would you like hot tea?"

"That would be great. I'm freezing." Penelope wanted to get up, to get her own tea. "I don't want to be waited on."

How could she find a new life if this was always going to be her story: people waiting on her, treating her like the heiress, the woman who couldn't take care of herself.

"I know you don't want to be waited on." Wilma lifted the teapot from the top of the stove and poured amber liquid into a tiny, porcelain cup. "Honey, you're hurt. When you're able, I know you'll help out around here. And the more you rest, the sooner that will be. You'll let the men go fishing tomorrow."

"Do you plan to stay here long?" Penelope hadn't meant to push or to pry. But the simple question made Wilma turn away, wiping her hands on her apron.

"I'm not sure yet. We're still searching for..."

Searching for what? The way back to Treasure Creek? No, she thought they all knew the way back. But she took Tucker's advice and she didn't push. Whatever the Johnsons were going through, it was obviously a difficult situation.

It made Penelope's situation look simple, easy. Her dad had picked a wealthy man as a suitable match for her. Most women would probably love to have her problems. It was hard for her to consider it a problem when she looked at what the people in Treasure Creek were going through. Amy had lost her husband. People's businesses were struggling. Tucker hadn't reached his father before he died. The Johnsons, she didn't know their story, but she knew the wounded look in their eyes.

Prayer was new to her life. It had happened back in Treasure Creek, at the back of the little community church, while the congregation sang a song of redemption. She had found faith, found God and found something that finally filled the emptiness that she had tried for years to fill in other ways.

"Would you like to help me peel potatoes?" Wilma set the cup of tea in front of her. "I mean, after you drink your tea. I thought we might have potato soup for dinner tonight. Instead, we'll fry potatoes to go with the fish."

"Of course I can help." She'd never peeled a potato in her life, but she could do it.

Wilma smiled. "That's wonderful. I'll get things ready and we'll peel potatoes and talk."

Penelope sat back in her chair, the warm cup of tea held in her hands. She watched Wilma scurry around the kitchen, pulling things from drawers and cabinets, not at all upset by the lack of electricity or running water. Penelope tried to picture her own mother in this kitchen, doing these things. The image didn't work.

Penelope's mother had never "roughed it." The surprise would be that Penelope had. But her adventures were her business.

"Here you go, a knife and potatoes." Mrs.

Johnson set a bowl on the table. "To put them in after they're peeled."

Penelope picked up the knife and the first potato. *Okay, not a problem. Peel the potato.* She glanced across the table at Wilma, who had a potato in her hand and was circling it with the knife. *Easy-peasy.*

The first potato disappeared with the peel. The five-inch spud turned into a three-inch dagger-looking thing. She'd do better on the next one.

She chopped it up and tossed it in the bowl and then reached for the next potato.

"Haven't cooked much?" Wilma chopped her potato into the bowl.

"Not much at all. I can make a mean cup of single-pod coffee."

"That's a skill." The male voice behind her was laced with sarcasm. She shifted and shot him a look that was also considered a skill.

He didn't wither.

Instead, he laughed a little. The sound was as delicious, maybe more so, than the cup of coffee she'd been dreaming about a moment earlier. Smooth, a little sweet, and it could warm a person down to the middle. She turned back to the potato she held and he stepped closer.

"Leave some of the potato behind and we'll

consider you a pro," he teased with a smile that matched the laugh.

"Thanks, I'll remember that."

Tucker crossed the kitchen with the bowl of fish. Penelope lifted her gaze to watch. She watched him pour water over the fish, and then he poured it over his hands. Without turning, he tended the stove. He shoved pieces of wood onto the embers, poked them, watched as they flamed and then closed the door.

When he turned to face them his face was ruddy from the wind outside and the heat of the stove. His sandy brown hair distracted her, because it was a shade darker than the beginnings of a beard that covered his jawline.

Why, oh why did a man's mouth look like that when it was framed by whiskers?

"Something on your mind?" He winked, then reached into a drawer, pulling out a paring knife.

"Nope." She anchored her attention back on the potato-peeling business and ignored the sigh from Wilma.

Tucker pulled out the chair next to her and sat down. Sat down, his shoulder close to hers, his scent all masculine and outdoors sifting around her, blending with the wood smoke.

"Why are we peeling potatoes? Didn't you

have faith in our ability to bring home fish?" He shot the question at Wilma.

"Of course I had faith. But I also have the good sense to be prepared." Wilma smiled sweetly and kept peeling. "And potatoes are always good. Rather than the soup I planned, I'll fry them. Where's that husband of mine?"

Tucker shrugged. "Saw him out by the shed."

Noncommittal. Penelope wondered what he wasn't saying. For a lawyer, he was a man of few words. Maybe that was for the best.

But why did he need to be noncommittal about Clark being near the woodshed? There were too many secrets floating around here, and not just hers. She'd seen the two men earlier that morning walking around the side of the house, pointing at something. When she'd peeked out the front door they scuffed around in the snow and headed back to the wood they'd been chopping.

Chapter Five

Tucker watched the women peel a few potatoes and then made the excuse that he needed to do something outside. What he needed was a few minutes of not sharing space with people. More specifically with a person.

He found Clark outside, looking off into the woods, his cap pulled low, with the flaps covering his ears. The older man turned, his eyes dark and troubled in a face that was weathered and worn. But he smiled more these days. Tucker wondered if it was about faith? The older couple had been bitter when he first showed up here at their hideaway.

They'd welcomed him, of course, but they'd been hurting and looking for a way to get back to faith. Because they had trusted God and thought He had let them down.

Tucker hadn't really blamed his pain on

God. He had blamed himself, thinking he should have been able to do something. He should have done what needed to be done—for his dad. For a young girl whose life was taken too soon. He should have done more to protect them, not done more for himself.

He stood next to Clark, sighing and breathing in frigid air. Dusk was already falling and the gray sky was getting darker.

"Who do you think is out there?"

Tucker shrugged. "Not a clue, but it has something to do with her."

"Yeah, the two kind of showed up together."

Penelope and trouble seemed to go hand in hand.

"I'll give her ankle a few more days to heal and then I'll have to walk her out of here. I guess I can't run from my life forever."

Clark nodded, he flashed Tucker a quick look and then his gaze shot back to the woods. "I know. We've been out here for half of a year. Half a year of praying and trying to find peace. Our son was going to serve God, and instead God took him. I keep thinking about all of our prayers going unanswered. I know better, Tucker, I know God wasn't ignoring us. And for years I've preached a good sermon about God's will and finding peace in His will. But here I am…"

"Human?"

Clark smiled when he looked at Tucker and Tucker felt a lift in his own spirits. He gave God some credit for the plane engine failing at just the right minute for him to land in the lake close to this cabin. He didn't know where he'd have gone if that hadn't happened.

"Tucker, I've been angry with God for a good long while. Or hurt. I guess I felt like a friend let me down. A friend I've always trusted."

"I get that." Hadn't he felt a little of the same when his mom left them?

"Wilma and I keep praying, trying to decide what to do. It's been hard, thinking about going back to the mission field."

"So you're going back when I take her out of here?"

"We'll discuss it and let you know."

"I'm not crazy about leaving the two of you out here alone." Tucker couldn't look at Clark, but he knew Clark would smile.

"We won't be alone."

"I guess you won't." Tucker shoved his hands into his pockets and tried not to think about feeling alone. He'd never been more alone in his life than the day he realized his dad wouldn't be calling him anymore. He would never have another chance to make amends.

What a crazy way to leave things, with anger over his dad choosing to buy a home in Treasure Creek. Stubborn. They'd both had a hand in the rift. They'd both been stubborn and unwilling to yield.

"Tucker, the pain doesn't last forever." Clark must have guessed his thoughts. The older man was good at that, at reading Tucker's expression.

"Sure."

"I guess you wouldn't believe me if I said that someday you'll look back and see what God was doing with all of this mess."

"Yeah, well, I haven't had my 'aha' moment yet, if that's what you're talking about."

"You could call it that."

Tucker pushed down a load of guilt and anger, mixed in with a reasonable amount of pain. Those were the moments he was having, and there was nothing 'aha' about it. Two people had died. One that he should have been there for. One that he hadn't known.

"Do you think we'll be able to get Penelope back to Treasure Creek?" Clark asked as he turned back to the house with Tucker following.

The two of them walked slow in the cool night air. "Does that mean you're going?"

"If we go, I should have said."

"We'll have to go slow. The road should be less than three days' walk. From there we can probably get a ride."

"We have the tent, plenty of food and warm sleeping bags. We'll have to carry quite a bit of our supplies."

"I have a good pack. Hopefully, this weather will hold."

"We can pray."

"Yeah."

"Fish for dinner?" Clark climbed the stairs, pausing on the porch to wait for Tucker.

Tucker turned his attention back to his friend. "Yeah, fish and potatoes."

"I thought I smelled something good." Clark opened the front door. "I don't know if our guests are still around, but let's keep the women inside unless we go out with them."

"Probably a good idea."

"I'll be in shortly."

Clark stood in the doorway, letting out a small shaft of yellow light from one of the lanterns in the hall. "Wilma will put your plate on the stove."

"She doesn't have to."

"But she will."

The door closed with a soft thud. Tucker stood on the porch, looking out into the darkened woods. Nothing but silence, the occasional screech of a bird or some other wild animal and emptiness. It should have made him feel alone. Instead he felt a presence that settled over his heart, pushing at him to acknowledge something long forgotten that had been buried so deep inside him that he'd stopping thinking about it—about faith.

He closed his eyes and tried to remember the first time he'd prayed, and the last. He could remember the first, when Mrs. Parker had asked him to pray at the end of a Sunday school class. The last? He couldn't remember, but he thought it was the day he came home from school and found the note from his mother, telling them she'd found someone else, someone who could give her the life she'd always dreamed of.

He opened his eyes, angry with himself for going back to that moment, to feeling like that kid again. He walked off the porch and breathed in the ice-cold air, letting it settle in his lungs and hoping it would clear his mind.

He wasn't that kid.

And people inside the house were expecting him to help get them to Treasure Creek.

He peered into the woods, knowing that he wouldn't see anything, or anyone. Maybe they were gone by now. Maybe they'd been looking for something other than Penelope Lear.

That didn't add up, though. There wasn't much else to find in these woods. And if a person was lost, they'd ask for help. Someone lost would ask for shelter.

The door opened. He turned and it was Penelope. She hobbled across the porch, silent for a moment, staring up at the now dark night sky.

"The stars don't shine like this in the city." She sounded breathless, a little amazed.

"No, they don't." He walked up the steps and stood next to her.

He looked up at the clear night sky and the millions of stars that glittered like diamonds in the velvety darkness. He'd missed this, missed the silence and the peacefulness of Alaska.

He grew up just a short distance from Treasure Creek. He didn't want to let the memories in—of his dad, fishing, and sometimes Jake showing up, to go on the boat with them. He'd been all too glad to leave it behind, to leave his dad behind. He'd been glad to leave hard times behind.

And yet here he was, back at home. He

could have gone back to Seattle after the funeral. He could have buried himself in work. He'd picked the Alaskan wilderness. Maybe because it reminded him of his dad.

"Are you going to eat?"

"In a few minutes. I was just enjoying…" The peace and quiet, by himself.

"Being alone." She turned, looking up at him. Blond hair catching the silver moonlight.

Tucker took a smart step away from her, away from temptation.

"Being alone is nice," he admitted, smiling a little because she had read him so easily.

"But I crashed your alone party?" She leaned against the post and looked out at the woods, away from him.

"Yeah, you did."

"Sorry." She glanced his way with a smile that he didn't think showed remorse. "Or maybe I'm not. I love it here."

"I hope you're feeling up to a little bit of a journey and a real chance to prove what you're made of."

"What do you mean by that?"

"In the next few days, as soon as your ankle is ready for travel, we're heading out."

"Walking?" Her eyes were wide, dark orbs in a pale face.

"How else?"

"We could find the Jeep?"

"Which is where?"

"I don't know." Her voice raised a little, got a little higher in pitch.

"Well, I have an idea, why don't you let Clark and me take care of the travel arrangements."

"That's the problem, your plan includes walking for days in the cold. It's Alaska and it's November. Or has that little detail been forgotten?"

"Rather self-righteous for a person who went off by herself after a treasure no one is positive exists."

"I was trying to help people."

"Now I'm trying to help you." And ignore the way her lips pursed and her eyes sparked like dark blue fire. *Redirect, Your Honor.* If he'd been in court, he would have redirected—his thoughts, her words, her look. "Weren't you the person who wanted to prove herself?"

The wind picked up, cold and out of the north. She shivered and huddled down into what he thought was probably very little warmth. They'd have to find her more suitable clothing for the trip out.

"So we'll walk out. Fine."

"I thought you'd be thrilled at the prospect of getting back to civilization."

"I think I'm doing just fine here. I'm actually enjoying myself. I'm not weak or a sissy."

"So you don't have any desire to get back to town, to electricity and to running water?"

Her chin came up at a stubborn angle. "No, I'm not in a hurry to get back. I could live off the land if I had to."

He laughed. "You couldn't fight your way out of a wet paper bag."

"That isn't true. I caught more fish than you. I could learn to shoot a gun and cook... game, or whatever."

His laughter faded because he couldn't laugh in the face of such an outrageous and obstinate protest from a woman wearing fuzzy boots.

She quickly looked away, but not before he saw shadows. He felt bad for baiting her. She was just as on the run as he was. Maybe more so. At least he was making his own decisions.

"Don't worry, we won't be there for a few days. I promise that after three days of pretty serious roughing it on the trail, you'll have proven yourself. And you'll be ready for Treasure Creek. You'll probably be ready to climb in your dad's jet and fly back to Anchorage."

"Thanks for thinking so highly of me." She turned and walked away, still limping, but her back was stiff and unyielding.

He was arrogant, and every other word he'd ever been called. He could have told her, had she waited to hear it, that he didn't even think highly of himself.

It wouldn't have hurt him to tell her that he admired her, that she was brave. He figured she'd been testing herself on that for years, just to prove it to a world that never noticed. No one noticed but herself.

And probably him. But he didn't want to notice.

He stalked off the porch and across the rough yard of the cabin. Ten minutes alone. He needed those ten minutes to tell God why he was still angry and why he wasn't ready to leave this cabin and the isolation of the Alaskan wilderness. He resented being forced to return to Treasure Creek, and he resented the intrusion of a woman who was determined to poke her nose into his life.

He glanced up at the dark sky, and to the north. Wisps of white and lavender light swirled in the night sky. The northern lights.

Where was God? When his mom walked out; when his dad held onto faith and Tucker couldn't; when his dad was dying and stubbornness kept the two of them from talking. Where was God?

When Anne died.

He let out a deep breath, and he wanted to hurt someone. He hadn't known her, but her death had changed his life. Because if it hadn't been for him, she would still be alive. Her parents would still have her.

If he wanted, he could make a big, long list of why he didn't need God. And he ignored the push, the voice that told him to write down a list of reasons he needed God.

The front door of the cabin opened again. He expected Clark. It was Penelope again. She stood in the lamplight, her hair brushed gold by the flame of the lantern she held.

It wasn't Christmas yet, but she reminded him of Christmas. She reminded him of twinkling lights, candy canes, the first snow. And annoying music. The kind that started out okay, but after a while it got under your skin.

He added the last as a final grasp at sanity. Fortunately, she turned and went back inside.

Maybe she hadn't seen him. Maybe she decided to leave well enough alone. Either way, he was grateful the door closed.

Penelope helped Wilma wash the dishes. Clark had eaten and gone off by himself. Penelope thought he spent time each evening in prayer. Tucker still hadn't come inside. Or if he had, he hadn't shown his face to claim the plate of food left warming on the stove for him.

The water in the bowl was lukewarm and even the rinse water was a little sudsy and gray. She dipped the clean plate that Wilma handed her, and then dried it and set it on the counter. Her mind slipped back to Treasure Creek and the small community church that she'd attended. She thought back to Amazing Grace and how it had felt to find faith, to fill the emptiness in her life with something that had seemed to be missing for as long as she could remember. Faith. That missing ingredient. She thought it was missing in Tucker's life, too.

"He's stubborn." She whispered as she dried the next plate.

She hadn't meant to think out loud. Wilma glanced her way with a curious smile and went back to the dishes. The older woman washed a coffee cup and handed it to Penelope to be rinsed.

"Are you grumbling about Tucker?"

"Yes." Penelope dried the cup. "Yes, I am. He's stubborn. He's like my father, my brother and all of the other men that I know. He's obsessed with control and with work. He's driven by his need to succeed. He thinks he can make decisions for everyone around him."

Wilma clucked a little. "He's driven, but he's good at heart. He's finding himself, finding that part that he lost a long time ago."

"He'd better hurry."

"We all need time, Penelope. We need time to adjust, to find ourselves, to find faith and to find our path in life."

"But you and Clark, you have faith. You know where you're going."

Wilma smiled, soft and a little sad. "We've struggled, too. It happens to all of us."

"What happened?" Penelope let the question rush out. "I'm sorry, that was wrong of me. A few days of knowing you doesn't give me the right to barge into your life."

"It isn't something we're hiding from." Wilma squeezed water from the dish rag and draped it over the now empty bowl. She sighed. "I guess we're not hiding from it. We were trying to outrun our sadness. Let's have cocoa."

"I'll heat the water." Penelope picked up the pitcher of water on the counter and filled the teapot.

"You're getting very good at this."

"I have to admit, it isn't second nature. Second nature would be turning on the faucet and heating water up in the microwave." Or having someone else do it for her.

"Yes, but there's something about this life, about doing things in a way that isn't easy, that makes a person grow."

Penelope put the teapot on the stove. She had watched Clark tend the fire inside the stove and she opened the door now to see if it needed more wood. It didn't.

"I hope I'm growing." She turned, staying next to the stove, leaning against the counter. The room smelled of wood smoke and the fish they had fried.

"You are. This is a good place to test your mettle, see what you're made of."

"I'm not sure if I'm made of much."

Wilma sat down at the table. "You're made of the best our good Lord has to offer. You're the finest metal and you're being tested now. He's put you in the fire and you'll come out better for it. We've been there, girl. We've been there."

The teapot whistled. Penelope poured water over cocoa in the cups, stirred the contents and moved to sit at the table with Wilma. They sat across from one another in that simple kitchen lit by candles and lanterns, cocoa in front of them.

"We lost our son." Wilma's eyes sparkled with unshed tears, and then a few of those tears dripped down her cheeks. "We were in Germany, he was in New York working. When we learned that he'd been hurt, we prayed and prayed. He was the child God had given us when we thought we would never have children."

"He must have been very special."

"He was." Wilma smiled a little, but her pain was evident in her eyes.

Penelope breathed in past the tightness in her chest. She was new at faith and didn't know how to say it easily, that she'd pray, or even that she understood. She'd never gone through anything that tore her heart out.

Her life felt shallow. She squeezed her eyes closed and thought back to all of the things she'd done to try to make her life matter— the charity work, the foundations, and then traipsing off to Treasure Creek, as though an adventure could fix it.

And the Johnsons had been giving up everything for God.

"I'm so sorry." She reached to cover Wilma's hand with her own.

"Thank you, Penelope." Wilma wrapped her fingers around Penelope's hand that still covered hers. "Aiden lived until we got to New York, and then he left us. Our only child. It's amazing, our story and Tucker's. God brought us together here, all three of us running from something."

"And then I showed up."

"And you're running, too, aren't you?"

Penelope sipped the cocoa and she didn't know how to answer. She thought about Tucker losing his father and the Johnsons losing their son. They had real problems to run from and real needs for God to meet. She was running from life and from marriage. She was running to find herself.

"I'm running, but I feel selfish now, because my life has been so easy."

"Honey, when it is our pain, it counts. Whatever we're going through, we're the ones going through it, and if it hurts, it hurts."

"Then it hurts." Penelope set her cup down. "But I'm praying that God has an answer."

"He always does. You don't pray that He has an answer. You pray that you'll recognize and accept the answer. That's the real hard part of faith."

Footsteps in the hallway ended their conversation. Penelope looked up as Tucker entered the room. He captured her gaze and held it, and she couldn't look away.

She watched as he picked up the plate that Wilma had set on the wood stove. He grabbed a fork out of the drainer on the counter and stirred his potatoes, tasting them before adding more salt.

Penelope focused on her cocoa. She took a sip, pretending he didn't matter and his opinion of her didn't matter. He carried his plate and sat down next to her.

It was definitely time to head out away from Tucker. She didn't want him to be her problem. And he'd fixed that for her. In a few days they'd leave. And a few days after that, they'd be in Treasure Creek. That meant getting away from him. She told herself she looked forward to parting ways with him.

She was more than positive he'd be ready to rid himself of her. She had crashed into his seclusion and she was the reason he had to return to Treasure Creek.

Chapter Six

They left at dawn three days later. Tucker looked back at the cabin that had been his refuge for the last few months. He'd been running from life. He looked at the three people following him. He hadn't escaped. Instead, he'd been pushed into three other lives, with no possible escape in sight.

Life had definitely found him.

The biggest problem was that the time away hadn't solved a thing for him. It had given him time to rest up and to enjoy nature, but it hadn't solved problems he left Treasure Creek with.

He still felt guilty. He still felt like the worst excuse for a son and a person.

The pack on his shoulders was a heavy weight, but nothing like the one he was heading back to Treasure Creek with. His attention landed on Penelope Lear and he came pretty close to smiling.

Wilma had found clothes in a closet. So Penelope had gone from fashion plate to homeless chic.

She was using a walking stick that Clark had made for her. Her feet were shoved into heavy snow boots and she was wrapped in an ancient parka that smelled of mothballs and musty closet.

At least she was warm.

He pushed on, refusing to look back. They had a long way to go. They also had company. He had seen the footprints again that morning. He'd tried to convince himself they were his footprints, but he didn't have shoes with that tread on the sole.

"How far will we walk today?" Penelope asked, and he shrugged. He figured this would be an adventure, with her asking "how much farther" on a regular basis. It would be worse than traveling with a five-year-old.

"Penelope, we'll walk as far as we possibly can." He looked up at blue skies. "This weather might not last. I want to make the most of it."

"You don't have to snap." She trudged on, her nose and cheeks pink and her eyes watery from the cold.

"I wasn't snapping." He sighed, because he *had* snapped. "I'm sorry."

"Thank you." She walked faster, catching up with him.

She walked by his side, her breathing soft and her steps quick to keep up with his. He looked down and shook his head. No wonder her dad wanted to marry her off. Herman Lear wanted her out of his home so he could have peace and quiet.

"Excited to be going back?"

"Sure." She didn't look up, but kept her gaze on the trail and on her feet as she walked.

"You don't sound excited."

She looked up and then back down, careful over the rocky path. There were slick spots and the best going was next to the stream. He just hoped none of them fell in. That would be a little more adventure than any of them needed.

"I'm not excited. I mean, I'll be glad to get back, but this hasn't been terrible."

No, she had something there. It hadn't been terrible.

"You're right, it hasn't been bad."

"You're probably not happy to be going back." She slid a little on ice and he grabbed her arm to steady her.

"What does that mean?"

"You were content to hide out there, away from your life and problems. You lectured me about staying put when you're lost, and yet you walked away from the plane."

The kitten had some pretty sharp claws. He would have smiled, but her words stung a little. She was insinuating that he ran from his problems. He'd never run from anything, never. Until June.

"I didn't run." He half attempted a denial and then he sighed. "I'm not excited."

Anything but excited. He would have to face Jake and Gage, who appeared to be about the only real friends he had in the world. He glanced back and the Johnsons were trudging a short distance behind, hand in hand. He had friends.

He noticed their red faces and slowing steps. He'd have to take breaks for their sake. If he hadn't worried about their safety at the cabin, they could have waited for the next supply drop and signaled the pilot.

When they got back to Treasure Creek they all had things to face. Penelope wasn't as free as she wanted him to think.

They walked on in silence. Penelope didn't talk. Sometimes her lips moved and he guessed that she was praying. He remembered that new faith, when knowing God was as new as falling in love for the first time. He'd been a kid, but he'd wanted to tell everyone who would listen.

He glanced up at the bright blue sky and then around him, at towering mountains and evergreens. They were following the stream because it would take them to a village inhabited by native Alaskans. That was a twenty-plus mile walk by his estimation. He knew that there was a fork in the stream when they reached that village, and taking the southern fork would lead them to Treasure Creek. They'd also be able to have shelter for a night. But that wouldn't happen for a couple of days. His hope was that someone in the village would give them a ride to Treasure Creek.

He pulled back his thoughts, because they had to take one day at a time and not get overanxious about making it to civilization. They had limited daylight and rough terrain to take into account. This day would end with the four of them camped along this stream, hoping a fire, their tent and sleeping bags would keep them warm enough. And he was pretty doubtful.

At least Clark and Wilma would have each other. He glanced down at the woman walking next to him, huffing with exertion, her cheeks glowing from the cold and exercise. He shook off thoughts of her in his arms, because that wasn't going to happen.

He wasn't about to play into her father's plan.

They set up camp before the sun went down. Penelope held a pole for the tent, which was about all the help she could be. Her fingers, even though she'd worn heavy gloves, were frozen and numb. Her cheeks were wind-burned and cold. She stumbled a little and Tucker shot her a look. He opened his mouth and then closed it. Good thing he did, because she wasn't in the mood to be lectured.

She glanced toward Wilma, who was steadily adding wood to the fire. Clark was stirring up some type of dried beef and vegetables with water. Soup. If only they could have coffee. She'd give anything for coffee. But Tucker had insisted on downsizing, and the coffeepot had been deemed too bulky to take along.

She was going to miss that blue coffeepot that had bubbled so cheerfully on the wood stove back at the cabin. She was going to miss the cabin. She'd gotten to be herself, just herself, for the first time in a long time.

"Hold that steady," Tucker commanded

as he tapped one of the last stakes into the ground. "Almost done."

She nodded but she couldn't talk. Her lips were frozen in a tight line. She trembled inside her coat, shivering until her back ached.

"Are you going to make it?" Tucker rounded the tent and was suddenly at her side.

"Of course."

"You look a little lost. Food will help." He took her by the arm and steered her toward the fire. "And heat."

"Yes, heat." She stood in front of the fire and soaked up its warmth. It left her back cold, so then she turned.

"This is a little more of an outdoor experience than you probably planned for."

"A little." She waited for Tucker to walk away. He didn't. He stood next to her for a long time and she wished he'd put an arm around her.

Sign of hypothermia. She'd read books. She knew the symptoms. People did crazy things when they got too cold. Sometimes they wanted to be held. And she'd never wanted to be held so badly in her life. Tears were burning her eyes and her throat tightened.

"Two more days, Penelope. You can make it." His voice was soft and close to her ear.

She nodded, but she couldn't get words

past the lump of emotion. He believed she could make it. He believed. She buried her face in her hands. How many people had ever believed she could make it?

"You're okay." His arm slipped around her waist. Before she could really think about it, she turned into the solid wall that was his chest. Her cold cheeks met warm flannel that smelled of the outdoors. Strong arms wrapped around her and held her close.

"Shhh, it's okay." He gathered her closer and she nodded, but she didn't want to talk, didn't want to move out of the safety of his embrace. She was suddenly in a place where it was okay to be weak, and yet someone thought she was strong.

"I'm sorry." She hiccupped the words and didn't move her cheek from the soft flannel of the jacket he wore under his coat.

"You're fine. You're strong. It's overwhelming out here, Penelope. It's cold. It's quiet. It's hard going. We're all tired. You're tired."

She pulled back and wiped her gloved hand across her cheeks. He took her hand in his and pulled the glove off and shoved it into the pocket of her coat and pulled the other off.

"I'll freeze without them." She started to reach into her pocket but he grabbed her hands, both of them, and held them tight in his.

"Your hands will freeze if you keep them on." He lifted her hands to his mouth and blew warmth onto her numb fingers. "This will help. After you get warmed up you can put them back on."

She could only nod. How could she do or say anything when this moment wrapped around her, stealing her breath, her thoughts and maybe even her heart.

"I should help do something." She backed away from him, immediately missing his warmth. Her hands wanted to be back in his. She wanted his arms around her again.

But moving away from him was the right thing to do. Even if it left her cold from the inside out.

She turned to Wilma, who was warming something in a pan and pretending she hadn't witnessed a moment of weakness between the two of them. Penelope justified it in her mind, telling herself that it was natural in this environment, in their circumstances. Of course they would be drawn to one another in this situation.

"What can I do to help?" She glanced back at Tucker and then she faced Wilma with a smile. She heard Tucker walk away and she breathed easier.

"Get our four mugs from the pack that Clark carried. Tucker said no coffeepot. He didn't say a thing about the soup pan I brought. Or the bag of instant coffee."

"Oh, Wilma, you're a blessing."

"I think so." Wilma smiled up at her. "Rehydrated soup and instant coffee. Not exactly a gourmet meal.…"

"It'll be the best meal I've ever had." Penelope rushed the words.

She watched Tucker carry sleeping bags into the tent. Three of them. He kept his outside. She started to ask why, but then she thought better of it. Two more days and they'd part ways. She wouldn't have to think about Tucker. He wouldn't have to think about her.

That would be better, she thought.

"Hold those mugs out, I'll pour our coffee." Wilma brought her back to planet Earth.

The aroma of the coffee, even instant, was wonderful. Penelope held the cups and Wilma poured from the saucepan. Clark appeared and he took the first cup with a smile.

"My wife is always up to a challenge." He winked at Wilma.

"Stop that, you crazy man." Wilma blushed

in the soft light of the fire. Her eyes lit up, though. Penelope wondered what that was like, to have someone who loved her that much. She wondered if she would ever know.

She thought about her mother, the way her mom's eyes looked when Penelope's dad entered a room. She shuddered to think about that being her life. She wanted someone like Clark, someone who held her tight and went through the hard things at her side.

Tucker took the cup of coffee she held out to him and she couldn't stop herself from thinking back to being held tight just five minutes earlier. Their gazes met and she thought he was thinking the same thing.

Tucker wasn't too upset with Wilma for packing the instant coffee. By midnight, with everyone sleeping in the tent and him parked next to the fire, he'd be real glad for a cup of coffee. He'd never been fond of the instant stuff, but when the temperature dropped to well below freezing, instant coffee wasn't so bad.

Mud heated up in water wouldn't have been bad.

He pulled his blanket around his shoulders and hunched down, with his back against an upturned log. One of his last nights of solitude. He wasn't sure how long he'd stay in

Treasure Creek, once he got back to town. Maybe a few days.

He had to go back to Seattle. The thought settled in the pit of his stomach and stayed there. For the first time in years, he wasn't excited about his job. He had always loved the challenge, the arguments, learning how people ticked, and what would make them say what he needed them to say.

Each time he closed his eyes he thought about an unknown girl, a family grieving. His grief.

The zipper on the tent ripped the stillness of the night. He turned, watching the dark figure hurry across the open area to the fire. She had wrapped her sleeping bag around herself and pulled on the boots he'd made her wear. She hadn't liked leaving the other boots behind.

He smiled, but quickly pushed that reaction down. This wasn't a friendship he wanted to pursue. Instead he stared up at her, wishing that look would send her running back to the tent.

The one thing he'd learned about Ms. Lear was that she didn't back down easily. Instead of cowering, she hunkered down next to him.

"I'm sorry I fell apart earlier," she whispered without looking up at him.

"No big deal." But it had been kind of a big deal, mainly because he still remembered holding her.

"I think I might have had a touch of hypothermia. The symptoms include confusion."

He laughed, at first loud and then softer. He didn't want to wake the Johnsons. If they could sleep, they should. Someone should get rest for the trip tomorrow.

"You think that was from hypothermia?"

She pulled the quilt tighter around her shoulders and moved so that her arm didn't touch his. "Of course. It isn't as if I'm prone to falling apart, or even to throwing myself into a man's arms."

"Of course you aren't."

"Stop."

"What?" The tone of her voice had changed to anger, taking him by surprise. "Why are you mad?"

"Because you insist on putting me in some little box that you've labeled 'heiress.' You think you know me, know how I should behave or what my life is like."

"I see." He knew the rule to this game. The less said, the better.

"You think I need a big, strong man to take care of me."

He listed off in his mind a few things,

starting with driving a Jeep off the road, leaving the Jeep to wander in the woods, coming face-to-face with a bear. He kept the list to himself while she rambled on.

"I'm sick of people like you."

"Okay."

"Stop."

"Penelope, I stopped talking a long time ago."

She peeked up, the sleeping bag tight around her neck so that just her face stuck out. Man, she had a kissable mouth. She had eyes that made him feel sucker-punched each time she looked at him all soft and vulnerable, or like a wildcat determined to fight her way out of a corner.

He leaned, and for the first time in a long time, he didn't think something through before he acted. As she stared up, half wildcat and half lost kitten, he leaned and touched his lips to hers. Soft at first, and then a little more demanding. He wrapped one arm around her quilted shoulders and held her close as his lips moved over hers. When she whispered his name and kissed him back, he didn't know if he'd ever breathe again.

Or if he'd ever want to breathe without her.

Her hair slipped through his fingers and he

held her close, leaning in for one more taste of the sweetest lips he'd ever kissed.

This was more tender than his first kiss with Cindy Douglas on the playground after school. It was sweeter than a college romance that he thought would last forever.

And it's smoke and mirrors, he told himself as he pulled away. She was just a mirage, something out of reach and unreal. He didn't need that. He didn't need this to cloud his thinking when so many things in his life were on the fence.

What he didn't need was a high-maintenance female in his life.

She obviously felt the same way about him, because she broke away from his arms and stood up, wobbling a little, scaring him because he wanted her away from the fire if she was going to trip. He reached but she backed up.

"Don't." She took a few more steps back. "This is just confusion from hypothermia."

He was tempted to laugh again, because she didn't believe that any more than he did. "Sure, hypothermia."

"Exactly. In a few days we'll be back to our real lives, being who we really are. And I don't think either of us would like the other person if we met up with them on the street."

"In the real world?"

"Exactly."

"I think I probably agree."

"Good night then." She turned, tripping a little over that crazy sleeping bag and then practically running to the tent.

That was the end of that. He almost relished the thought. But it wasn't the end. He had a bad feeling it wasn't even close. Maybe the bad feeling came from deep inside, where he didn't want it to be the end.

And as tired as he was—he must have been tired, or he wouldn't have thought that way—he was in for a long night. No way could he go to sleep and leave them vulnerable to whoever was prowling in the woods.

If there even *was* someone out there.

Penelope ran from a kiss that probably changed not only how she felt about Tucker, but how she felt about herself. Her heart raced and her fingers trembled as she climbed back into the tent and zipped the flap. As if zipping the flap would close out the cold. They had built a small fire a short distance from the tent, and their sleeping bags were supposed to be for near-arctic temperatures, but none of that seemed to matter.

After the warmth of Tucker's kiss, she felt cold to the bone.

She curled up in the sleeping bag and tried to count sheep, but sheep weren't enough. Clark was snoring, and outside, animals were making noises that sounded like grunts and sometimes growls.

Hours later, she thought something pawed around her corner of the tent. She huddled in a ball and prayed for it to go away. It continued to snort and dig. Clark snored louder, coughed a little and continued to snore.

She could see the flicker of the fire and watched as Tucker's silhouette moved, adding wood. He sat back down, wrapping himself in a sleeping bag. Tomorrow would be a rough day for all of them, but especially for Tucker.

It was all on him—to take care of them, to get them back safely. Clark was a big help, but it was Tucker who took charge and kept them going forward.

She closed her eyes and tried to slow her breathing to bring on drowsiness and maybe sleep. What a mistake. Closing her eyes intensified the noises inside and outside the tent. Closing her eyes meant remembering the softness in Tucker's eyes when he leaned to kiss her.

That meant remembering the way he'd slid his hands into her hair and pulled her close. Now what in the world was a girl supposed to do with those thoughts, with that memory?

She couldn't run far enough or fast enough to outrun how it had felt to be in Tucker Lawson's arms that way. The best thing she could do would be to remember that he was exactly the kind of man her father wanted her to marry, and the type she had no intention of marrying.

Chapter Seven

"Tromping through the cold, in a cold, white wonderland, over the mountain we go, freezing all the way. Ears so cold they ring, making my feet numb, oh what fun it is to walk…"

"Enough already!" Tucker turned and shot the chirpy socialite a glare that he hoped was colder than the ice in the stream they were walking next to.

She'd been making up words to the tunes of familiar Christmas songs for the last hour. Her cheerfulness was about to do him in. No one should be cheerful when they had walked for two days in the frozen Alaskan wilderness, and with no end of walking in sight. Either she didn't get how bad their situation was, or she was pretending everything was great.

His look went from Penelope to Wilma and then to Clark. The older couple was rock solid. Years in the mission field had conditioned them to some pretty tough conditions. They smiled at Penelope, who had stopped singing.

"I'm just trying to keep our spirits up and make time pass a little more quickly." She leaned on the walking stick as she trudged forward, limping. He let out a sigh and bit back any other angry retorts. She'd really proven herself out here. She hadn't whined or complained. She hadn't asked to stop for a break. Yet she was barely able to walk.

"Let's take a rest." He pulled the pack off his back.

"For real?" Her smile lit up her eyes.

"Yeah, Pollyanna, for real."

"You're such a charmer." She wrinkled her nose and walked away from him, right up to a fallen log that she lowered herself onto with a sigh. Wilma joined her.

"It's too early to make camp." He mumbled as he walked away, looking for dry firewood. He glanced up at the sky. Nearly two in the afternoon and the sun was dipping behind the mountains. The early dusk wasn't nearly as much of a problem as the clouds on the horizon. Gray, heavy clouds. The kind that dropped huge amounts of snow.

"We can't stop here." Clark looked at the

sky and then at his watch. "I don't remember how far that village is, but I think we can make it by dark. Or at least be there early tomorrow."

Another night in the cold. Another night without sleep. Tucker rubbed his hand across his face and nodded. He looked back to the women. "Yeah, I know."

"They're fine, Tucker."

Tucker nodded, but he wasn't so sure. He watched Penelope rub her ankle through the heavy boots she wore.

"What if I go on alone?" He turned back to Clark and the older man was already shaking his head.

"Not a good idea. You know as well as I do that sticking together keeps us safer and stronger. Think about headlines you've read. Someone always ends up hurt when people split up."

"Yeah, I know. But I don't know how much longer she can walk on that ankle."

"I know. But it's possible that we're just a few hours from the village."

"Okay, we'll break here and in thirty we're moving on."

Penelope had left the log and was heading toward them at a slow, hobbling pace. "Clark,

I'm new at this faith business, but something has really been on my mind."

"What's that, Penny?"

Tucker shot her a look. Just a few days ago she'd told him not to call her that. She didn't say a word to Clark, instead she smiled brightly and went on.

"We haven't prayed. I mean, I guess it's a given that God will take care of us, but…"

"Stop pushing, Penelope." Tucker glanced from her to the older man. She might not be willing to give people a break, but Clark and Wilma deserved one. And Penelope Lear probably hadn't gone through one tough thing in her life.

"Sometimes people need to be pushed, Tucker." Clark cleared his throat. "Sometimes we need to be reminded. I've spent the last few months looking for God, and ignoring Him every chance I got."

Tucker started to walk away, but Penelope Lear reached for his hand. Chipped fingernail polish was about the only remnant of her old life. Out here in the wilderness she was just as lost, just as cold as the rest of them.

She led him back to Wilma and the four of them joined in a circle. Tucker bowed his head, but as Clark prayed for direction, for health, for peace, Tucker thought about his dad, about a girl he'd never met, and about how his life had taken one big, wrong turn.

Amen.

It was dark and cold and it was only five in the afternoon. Penelope leaned on the walking stick and wished it actually helped. For a while it had. Now it seemed to take more energy to use it. And her hands were numb from cold.

She couldn't think of any more songs to sing.

She'd never wanted to be home more than she did at that moment. It hit suddenly—homesickness, wishing she could talk to her mom, and hoping they weren't worried sick. She hadn't meant to worry them.

"In the mountains we can build an igloo…" Tucker moved next to her. His voice was soft and held a hint of laughter. "Come on, Pollyanna, cheer up."

"I'm cheered," she whispered, but she couldn't smile, couldn't laugh. Pain felt like fire shooting up her leg.

"And pretend that it's a healing spa." Tucker nudged her a little and then slid his arm through hers and took part of her weight. "What comes after that?"

She shook her head. She wasn't going to

sing about snowmen and marriage. "I don't want to sing."

"Of course you do."

She closed her eyes and leaned against him. His arms tightened around her, holding her up, keeping her close. "I'm tired."

"I know you are."

They trudged on through the late afternoon. The temperature had dropped throughout the day and Penelope couldn't begin to imagine how cold it was. Without the sun to warm them it was miserable. Behind them, Wilma and Clark talked in quiet voices. They were tired, too.

"Come on, I'll give you a lift for a while." Tucker leaned in and spoke close to her ear.

"I'm fine, Tucker. We'll get there soon."

"You're not fine. Come on, Penelope." He pulled her to a stop and before she could complain he scooped her into his arms and held her close. "Isn't that better?"

"You'll get worn out carrying me. I really can walk."

"I'm strong."

He *was* strong, she knew that—and it was part of the problem. His strong arms around her, holding her close, that was a real problem. He made her imagination circle back around to the snowman in the meadow.

"Later on, we'll perspire, as we sit by a fire..." she sang.

"You want to perspire?"

"After being this cold, I'd be happy with sweating like a hog. Wouldn't my mother cringe if she heard that?"

"I'm sure she would."

"I really can walk."

"I know you can." He jostled her, moving her so that she was closer and her face was near his. She couldn't think of snowmen, instead she thought of last night.

"Hey, I see a light." Clark shouted. "Up ahead, see it?"

Tucker nodded and she held on to him as he picked up his pace. "Is it the village?"

"It is." Clark let out a whoop that belied his sixty years and Penelope laughed. She laughed until she cried.

"You can let me down now."

"Nah, I think I'll just carry you into camp."

"So everyone will think you're a big, strong man?"

He laughed. "No, they'll think we're married. I believe its an ancient wedding ceremony. It's a lot more effective than a snowman named Parson Brown."

Penelope struggled to get free but his grip tightened. "Let me down."

"I'm kidding, Penny. I promise you, carrying a woman into camp isn't a wedding ceremony."

"You're sure?"

"Nearly." He kissed the top of her head and snuggled her close.

Music drifted from the village. She could see Christmas lights, a fire and people. "People!"

He laughed. "You haven't been away from civilization for more than a week."

"It was a long week." She tried to count back, but she couldn't remember how many days it had been. Maybe more than seven.

"Yeah, it was."

She ignored him.

Wilma and Clark walked ahead of them. They'd been at the cabin since May. Months with no one to talk to but each other and Tucker. And then her. She thought about how much she'd miss them. She'd only known them a week, but they filled a space in her life. She and Wilma had talked about faith, about finding God. Wilma had shared about their pain when they lost their son, and how they'd felt like God let them down.

They'd spent six months finding peace with

God and with their lives. Yesterday Wilma told her they were ready to go back to the mission field, ready to continue on in what God had for them.

They were at peace because they knew that their son had known God, known faith.

Penelope glanced at Tucker, at the lines of his face in the dark. His mouth was set in a firm line. His eyes were on the village ahead of them.

She felt a funny tumble in her stomach at the thought of losing these three people. As soon as they got back to Treasure Creek they'd go their separate ways. They'd go back to the lives they'd been running from and from decisions they had to make.

She didn't want to lose them.

"Promise you'll call me sometime." She looked up at Tucker, biting her lip as she waited for his reply.

"Call you?"

"You know, on the phone. They have those in the real world."

"I know, but…"

"But you plan on walking away, going back to Seattle and forgetting you knew me. Don't you dare forget Clark and Wilma. They need you. You're their son now."

"How do you figure?"

"God put the three of you together after you lost your dad and they lost their son. God did that."

"Oh, God did that." His voice trailed off, as if he was considering it.

"Yes, and don't argue. You can forget me if you want, but you can't forget a couple that took you in and that you spent four months of your life with."

"I don't plan on forgetting them."

Them, not her. She nearly sighed. But they were spotted. Villagers were running toward them.

"What tribe is this?" She held tight to his shoulders as they moved closer to the village.

"I'm not sure. But it looks like we caught them in the middle of a celebration. It's November, Alaskan Native Heritage Month."

"I hope they don't mind visitors."

"I'm sure they've got several. This is more for outsiders than for them."

"I hope they have food."

"They'll have food."

People surrounded them, ending their conversation, ending their time together. Tucker didn't put her down, but then they were in the circle of light, near the fire and chairs. He sat her down as Clark explained who they were and where they'd been. Someone handed Tucker a phone and in the next few minutes she heard him talking to his friend Jake, explaining that both he and Penelope were alive, telling where they were.

From across the campfire she saw Tucker moved toward a group of men, and then Wilma hurried toward her, reaching Penelope just as the doctor removed her shoe.

It happened too fast, this reentry into life, into civilization. She was Penelope Lear again, and that was all that seemed to matter to anyone—her name.

Tucker accepted a cup of coffee after making a phone call to Jake in Treasure Creek. He'd been right about Herman Lear. He'd been using every resource imaginable to find his daughter.

He carried the coffee into the town's small gathering hall, where they'd taken Penelope and the Johnsons. From outside the frosty window, he could see her inside, sitting with her foot propped while some Dr. Single and Handsome talked to her, touching her foot, smiling. Penelope wasn't smiling though.

At that moment, Penelope glanced out the window and caught his gaze. What he saw in her eyes was that she was trapped, pure and simple. She looked like a scared kitten looking for a way out. She should have looked like a stray that had just been given a home and a bowl of milk. He let out a sigh as he pushed the door open and stepped into the wood-fire-heated warmth of the hall.

Electricity. Boy, he hadn't used that in a while: bright overhead lights and a radio blaring. He shuddered a little. It was going to take time, getting used to civilization. And he needed a haircut. He hadn't realized until he looked in a mirror just how shaggy his hair had gotten.

"How is she, Doc?"

Dr. Good Looks glanced up, not smiling. "She shouldn't have made that walk, but I think she'll be fine."

Man, this guy was serious. "No, she probably shouldn't have. But walking was better than the alternative."

Staying in the woods all winter. Worse, meeting up with whomever had been at the cabin.

He winked at Penelope and she nearly smiled. "Want a cup of coffee?"

She nodded. "I'd love one."

"See, Doc, that's all it takes. A cup of coffee, a good night's rest and she'll be back to her old self."

Back to being Penelope Lear. He watched her, wondering if being Penelope Lear was really any better than being Tucker Lawson.

"Your dad is coming here to meet you." He leaned against the wall. She glanced up, her eyes shadowed and a little tearful. "I'll go get that coffee."

"Thanks."

He wanted out of there before she cried. Tears weren't his thing. He glanced back over his shoulder at Penelope on the chair and the doctor sitting across from her now. Yeah, he was the kind of guy who could handle tears.

Tucker walked out into the cold Alaska night. In the center of the town a fire burned bright, and the village residents were performing a colorful dance, displaying their heritage for the few dozen people who had showed up for the festival.

"Tucker, hold up." Clark Johnson hurried across the street to catch up with him.

"Did you get Wilma settled at the pastor's home?" Tucker walked next to the older man. The ground was covered with a light dusting of snow and picked up the light of the full moon. It was cold though, deep-down cold.

"Yes, but she's heading across the street to check on Penelope. She isn't going to let you two kids go, you know. As far as she's concerned, you're both hers now."

"I don't think either of us is bothered by that."

"What will you do, Tucker?"

"What do you mean?"

"I know you have to settle your dad's estate. But are you going back to Seattle to your law practice?"

Tucker shrugged. "I don't know what else I'd do. What about you?"

"Back to Germany and our church there. Last spring we didn't know if we could do it again, but now...well, how can we not?"

"I guess I don't know how you can." Tucker paused for a moment to think about what he wanted to say. With anyone else he'd hold back. A quick look at him and he knew that Clark would want nothing but the truth. "You've given your life to serving God, and what did that get you?"

"Well, Tucker, it got us through a storm. It helped us heal. Our faith gave us something to hold onto. Yes, we were angry. We were hurt. We felt let down. We can feel those things and still have faith."

"I wish I had met you a long time ago, Clark."

"No such thing as too late, if that's what

you're thinking." Clark stopped walking. The snow was coming down hard, and in the distance Tucker heard the choppy sound of a helicopter. "Where are you heading?"

"Coffee for Penelope."

"How is she?"

"Good, I guess."

"I think she would have stayed out in the cabin all winter."

"I think she would have driven you crazy if that had happened." He knew she would have driven *him* crazy…or something.

Clark laughed. "No, she wouldn't have driven us crazy. Watching her come to life was like watching a child take their first steps. She's a pretty special young woman."

A sentence loaded with meaning, and Tucker wasn't biting. Clark and Wilma had fallen into the trap of matchmaking.

Instead of responding, he dug out the wallet that had been dormant for months. He still had cash, but he figured that his credit cards were probably frozen.

They walked to a small refreshment stand. Tucker strolled up to the Formica-topped counter and ordered coffee to go.

Suddenly lights flashed across the ground from a beam from the sky. He knew who was in that helicopter. He watched the lights skim across the night sky.

"Here's your coffee." The girl slid the cup across the countertop, but her eyes were on the helicopter. "Who do you think is riding in that? Did they have to call in a life flight for someone?"

"No, it isn't medical. It's here to pick some-one up." He picked up the cup of coffee.

People were running in the direction of the lot where the helicopter had landed. The blades were still beating the air. Probably the most excitement this village had seen in a while. Most of them probably didn't know who Herman Lear was, but it didn't matter much. The man had come to get his daughter.

Chapter Eight

The helicopter flew over, its spotlight hitting the snowy ground. Penelope shuddered and hunkered down in her coat. She wished she had that coffee Tucker had promised. She could really use the warmth of that coffee. A soft hand rubbed her back. She smiled up at Wilma.

"You'll be home in no time flying in that thing."

Penelope nodded. "I know."

"Oh, honey, they've been worried about you. Give them that pretty smile of yours."

"I'm not ready to go back home. I'm not ready to leave…" She sniffed. This was so embarrassing. "I'm not ready to leave you and Clark."

"Well, we aren't going to lose each other. I plan on seeing you every chance I get."

Penelope reached for Wilma's hand. "I won't let you forget that promise."

Outside the hall, people were running across the open lot. Penelope wouldn't have run, even if she could. Instead, she continued to watch that crowd, looking for a familiar face that she shouldn't have been looking for. She hadn't seen her parents in several weeks. She should have been looking for their faces in the crowd, thinking about them.

And she was. But thinking about her parents left her stomach unsettled, twisting in knots.

The face she'd been searching for appeared out of the dark shadows, stepping into the streetlight. He held a a cup of coffee. Tall, his shoulders were broad beneath his parka. The hood was pushed back. He was all man. She couldn't begin to picture him suited up in the courtroom. She liked him this way, in faded jeans, plaid and that big heavy parka. His hair was a little long, a little windswept. He hadn't shaved in days.

She wasn't cold anymore.

She wasn't afraid.

He walked through the door, bringing brisk air and the aroma of coffee. "Honey, I'm home."

She laughed a little and then tears started

to drip down her cheeks. She wiped them away, wishing she wasn't such a baby. Why in the world was she crying? She didn't have a reason to be sad. They'd made it out safely. She was going home. Tucker set the cup down on the table. She really wanted that coffee.

"Hey, why are you crying now? Tomorrow you'll be back in Anchorage having a spa day with the girls."

"Who said I'm going back?" The tears dried up and she sat a little straighter. "Seriously, who said I need spa days?"

"I just thought that after this, you'd be tired of adventure."

"Are you jetting off to Seattle tomorrow?"

"No, I have business to take care of in Treasure Creek."

"Well, so do I."

He handed her the cup of coffee and sat down in the chair across from her, moving her foot to the side a little. "Go home, Pollyanna. Go back with your parents. Let them take care of you. They've been worried sick. I talked to Jake and he said they had search teams, planes and helicopters looking for you."

"I know they've missed me. I know they were worried. I'm not selfish. I just…" She sipped the coffee before going on. "I love

Treasure Creek. I love being a part of that town."

"Seriously?"

"Yeah, seriously."

She loved walking down the street and being greeted by people. She loved the church bells that rang on Sunday mornings, and people telling her they'd pray for her. And they meant it.

But Tucker didn't want to hear a long, rambling explanation of why she loved Treasure Creek. Like every man in her life, he was ready to ditch her and get back to work.

She pulled her coat closer around her body and waited for her parents to reenter her life. The hall was brightly lit by overhead fluorescents that glared off the white tile floor. She blinked a few times and watched the glass door. Tucker stood up, patting her shoulder as he moved away. She could hear people talking outside. They were closer. And then she saw them hurry past the windows.

Tucker touched her arm. "Don't worry, I'm not going to forget you."

The door opened and her parents rushed in. Her mother was bundled in fur. Her father's black coat swished, dropping moisture as he entered the room.

"Penelope." Her mom pushed past him,

grabbing her up in a hug. Penelope hugged her back. She knew they loved her. She knew it. Their lives had just always been so busy.

As much as she'd told herself it wouldn't matter, she felt it suddenly, missing them and being glad for them.

"Mom, I'm sorry."

"What were you thinking?" Herman Lear's voice boomed. She looked up, meeting blue eyes the same color as her own. He didn't smile, he just shook his head as if he expected something like this from her.

What had she been thinking? It had been days since she'd made the plan. She'd been thinking that she, Penelope Lear, could single-handedly save Treasure Creek. And instead, she had to be saved.

She looked past her dad, searching the room for a familiar face. He was at the back of the crowd, near the door. When he winked, she smiled back and it felt good.

He wouldn't forget her. Maybe they'd even talk from time to time. She let herself believe he meant that. But didn't people always make those promises? She couldn't begin to name college friends that she'd promised to keep in contact with. Now she couldn't even remember their names.

"Let's go home." Her dad reached for her

arm. She stood, not putting weight on her ankle. "Easy, kiddo."

Kiddo?

"I can't go home." She accepted the crutches the doctor held out to her.

"You're going home."

"I want to go back to Treasure Creek. I left my stuff there. I have people I want to see."

"In that little town?"

"Yes, Dad, in that little town."

"Penelope, your life is not in that town. Your life is with us, and with a good husband."

"That you pick." This wasn't the way she wanted to spend a reunion with her parents, with her dad. He had that hard look on his face, the one he wore at the office. He was all business. People were watching, listening.

"I don't want to do this, Dad." She whispered with her head down, hoping they could at least get to the privacy of the helicopter.

"You haven't picked one for yourself."

Her gaze shifted to the man she'd spent the last week with. No, she hadn't picked. But she'd done a lot of praying and she'd done a lot of soul searching as she considered her future. She took a few steps. "Is there room for the Johnsons and Mr. Lawson to fly back to town with us?"

Her dad shrugged, as if it didn't matter.

"I suppose. Now, come on. Your mother is exhausted. She's been worried sick."

"I'm sorry." She looked around the room, with its two desks and scattered chairs. "Wilma, are you and Clark ready to go back to Treasure Creek?"

"Oh, no, honey." Wilma patted her arm. "We have a room for the night. We're staying with the pastor, and he's taking us back tomorrow. We're not in any hurry."

Penelope felt her heart lurch. She wanted them with her. Needed them. But she knew that Wilma needed to rest. It made perfect sense that they wouldn't want to jump into the helicopter and rush off into the night.

A hand touched hers. She turned, expecting her father, expecting anyone but Tucker Lawson. "I'll ride back with you."

"You don't have to."

"I know, but I'm ready to get back to Treasure Creek. When I talked to Jake, he kept going on and on about how great love is. I doubt I can talk him out of getting married, so I should at least be there for him."

"He's happy. This isn't some devastating event you have to nurse him through."

Tucker smiled a half grin and winked. "I know he's happy. More power to him, as long as it isn't catching."

"I'm afraid there's something contagious in Treasure Creek." But she wouldn't catch it either.

Tucker opened the door for her and they walked together into the cold night air, toward the waiting helicopter. Her parents hurried ahead of them, heads bent against the wind and steady fall of snow.

"Need me to carry you?" Tucker offered, and at first she thought he was joking, but he stopped and he looked as if he would really do it, as if he would pick her up and rush her toward the waiting helicopter.

"I'm good."

"Suit yourself."

She would suit herself. She told him so, and he laughed as they climbed the steps of the helicopter. Once inside, they were separated by her parents. She glanced in his direction, but he was looking out the window. He was already forgetting her.

The helicopter landed in Treasure Creek. People waited a short distance away. Red lights flashed through the night sky. As they hurried down the steps, Jake rushed forward, toward them. Gage was a short distance behind. Tucker exhaled a huge sigh of relief. He was done running. Time to face…life.

"Buddy, we've been worried sick about you." Jake clasped his hand and then pulled him close in a bear of a hug, patting his back hard. "What in the world happened?"

"Long story, one I'll be glad to share. Tomorrow."

"That's good to hear, Lawson, because I need a full report." Police Chief Reed Truscott said, the city cop. Tucker nodded and shook the man's extended hand. "I know it's been a long three days, but tomorrow I'd like for you to stop by my office. We've had a lot of people searching for you."

"I'm sorry about that Reed. I know it cost the town, and I'll be glad to help with the expense." His gaze followed the retreating back of Penelope Lear as she was hustled away by her family. "I need to tell you about a problem we had out at the lodge."

"What's that?" Reed walked next to him, Jake on the other side. Tucker would prefer to talk about his friend's relationship with Casey. That would have to wait until the situation with Penelope was dealt with.

An oil man like Jake and a tomboy tour guide. Tucker shook his head and then pulled his thoughts back on the track they'd derailed from. "Someone was at the cabin. They showed up at about the same time as Penelope

Lear. I'm not sure what they wanted, and we never saw anything more than tracks, but I'm pretty sure it has something to do with her."

"We'll keep an eye on her." Reed's smile faded. "This treasure map situation has blown this town apart. I know Amy had good intentions when she talked to that reporter about Treasure Creek, and the people that article has brought into town have been a Godsend, but I could just about do without all the drama and the people trying to get their hands on that map."

"Why would you think this has to do with the map?"

"Well, everyone figured Penelope went off in search of that treasure. She got a look at the map and hightailed it out of here. Not that she needs a treasure."

"Exactly. So maybe whoever it was sneaking around decided it would be easier to take Penelope Lear for ransom than to search for a treasure that might not exist."

Jake whistled. "Wow, I wouldn't have thought of that."

Tucker shot his friend a look. "It makes sense to me."

"Maybe it's one of the men her dad targeted as a husband wanting to get an idea of what kind of trouble she'd be." Jake kind of laughed, but Tucker knew the truth. Old man Lear had approached Jake as well as Tucker.

"She isn't trouble, she's just…"

Reed and Jake both looked at him, waiting for him to finish. He didn't have a word to finish the thought. At least not one he wanted to share.

"She's high-maintenance," Jake supplied, his brows shooting up.

When was the last time he'd hit Jake? Tucker tried to remember. It seemed like they might have been about sixteen, and Jake had smarted off and grinned, a little like the way he was grinning at that very moment. Tucker clenched his fist and relaxed it. Jake was still grinning.

"I'm going to my dad's."

Reed stopped him. "I need more information about what happened out there, Tucker."

"Yeah, I can do that. Would tomorrow be okay? I haven't slept in a few days."

"Tomorrow would be good."

"Need a ride?" Jake offered as Reed walked away toward a patrol car that was idling near the fire station.

The town was lit with a few flickering streetlights and the full moon. It was a quaint little place, just a dot on the map now, but it had once been a boomtown. He had run as fast he could from these towns a dozen or so years earlier.

This had been the last place he wanted to be. The last place he wanted his dad to be. He had a bad habit of running from the things he didn't want to face. He'd run from his dad's broken heart. He'd run from his own guilt back in Seattle.

"I can walk."

"A mile? In this cold?"

"Yeah, I'll take a ride." Tucker followed Jake across the deserted street, past the community church where Penelope had found faith a couple of weeks earlier, and past Lizbet's Diner. Lights glowed inside the diner, just enough to leave it all in shadows. The white letters stood out on the darkened window.

Snow fell a little heavier. Tucker pulled the collar of his jacket up and picked up his pace. He was about ready to be warm. It felt as if it had been weeks since he'd really been warm.

"What happened out there?" Jake asked as they got into his waiting truck.

Tucker clicked the seat belt and shrugged. "What do you mean?"

"I mean, what were you looking for? What did you find?"

Not peace, that's for sure. "I don't know. Answers, I guess. And what I found was an older couple looking for God, and then Penelope showed up."

"Yeah, that's the part I'm wondering about. What happened to you out there?"

"Nothing happened. I didn't really find peace. And the last week has been a royal pain."

"I bet she has."

"This isn't about her. Look, I'm happy that you've relinquished your man card in favor of a happy-ever-after card, but don't try to take mine. I'm still happily single. I didn't bite that hook when Herman Lear called me, and I'm not biting now. There's more to her than I would have imagined. But I'm not husband material. I work a lot of hours, and when I do head in that direction, I'm looking for someone…"

He wasn't even sure what he was looking for anymore.

"Not pushing, Tucker. And believe me, I still have my man card."

"Good to hear." Tucker leaned back in the seat of the truck. Heated leather. "Man, I'm tired."

"I bet you are. You're crazy, too. I can't believe you went off like that."

"Me? At least I knew where I was going. I didn't hop in a Jeep and go hunting for buried treasure."

Jake laughed. "Penelope again?"

The way he said it bugged Tucker. *Yeah, Penelope again.* If he closed his eyes, he could picture her walking along that trail, huddled into her coat and limping, but singing Christmas carols.

He shook his head to clear the image, the way he used to shake an Etch-a-Sketch to undo a drawing. It didn't work, though. Instead, he could almost hear her singing "Silent Night."

Penelope tiptoed down the stairs of the bed-and-breakfast, slipped on her coat and slid out the door. It was still dark. She didn't mind. She'd lived in Alaska her entire life. Her ancestors had come here in the late 1800s and bought up land that later proved to be rich in gold and oil.

Her father had invested in tourism, which he considered the oil of the future. Penelope knew his business, how it operated and what it could do. When she tried to become a part of things he got bristly. That was his reason for the manhunt to secure her a nice husband who would provide for her needs and keep her at home, working on charity events.

People were up and around, even though it was barely six in the morning. She'd left a note on her bed for her parents. She wanted a cup of Lizbet's coffee and a cinnamon roll. She didn't want more questions or a lecture. She didn't want to face her dad when he said that it was time to go home.

It hadn't happened before in her life, but Treasure Creek had changed things for her. This felt like home. This community and its people had settled in her heart in a way she knew her family wouldn't understand.

Last night, when she tried to explain it to her parents, they'd cut her off. She didn't like that feeling, as if she were still a teenager and had no right to make her own choices. She wasn't going back to that world, or to hiding her life in secrets and lies.

She walked through the door of the diner and a bell jingled as the door closed. A few people shot curious glances her way. She waved at the morning waitress, Becca, as she slid into a booth and turned her cup over for the anticipated cup of coffee.

"Penelope, we worried that we weren't going to get you back." Becca pulled out her order pad. She smiled big, her dark hair pulled up in a spiky ponytail and her white blouse pressed free of wrinkles. She was young, maybe eighteen. Young enough to still have some acne. "What will you have this morning?"

"I want coffee, and I'm dying for a cinnamon roll."

Becca poured coffee, and the aroma lifted with the steam from the mug. "Here you go. So, was it rough out there? I mean, did you see wolves? Did you nearly freeze?"

"I got lucky and found shelter." Easy words for landing in the arms of Tucker Lawson.

And Becca wasn't fooled. The girl grinned. "Yeah, you found shelter. Tucker Lawson, that's pretty amazing to be stuck in the woods with him. Last night, when it was announced that he'd been found, you should have heard the uproar. Half of those fancy women that have come to town were positive they could steal him if he came back to town."

"The Johnsons were with us." Penelope assured the younger woman. "And the women are welcome to him."

"Yeah, but still."

"Nothing happened." Heat settled in Penelope's cheeks.

Becca's smile softened from teasing to kind. "Oh, I know it didn't. I was just teasing you."

"I know." Penelope stirred in creamer and sugar. "And it's good to be back."

"I'll get that cinnamon roll. I'll make sure it has extra frosting on it."

Penelope's mouth watered in anticipation.

When Becca walked away, she looked up and realized people were watching. A few were obviously talking about her. She folded her napkin and folded it again. They probably had questions similar to the ones that Becca asked.

Which meant it might be better to leave with her parents. She loved this place, but she didn't want to be the person everyone was talking about. At least in Anchorage she had her life, her safety zone.

It hurt, thinking of losing the life she had thought she'd found in Treasure Creek. She just wanted to be Penelope, someone people liked for herself, not for who she was.

The door of the diner opened. Penelope glanced up and smiled when Amy James walked in and headed in her direction. The other woman, older than Penelope by just a few years, smiled. Amy was one of her real reasons for finding faith. Penelope had never met anyone like the widowed mother of two. With everything happening to Amy, she still had faith. She still believed that God was going to do something big in her life and in her community.

Her faith had been infectious. From the first moment that Penelope met her, to the time when Amy gave a brief testimony in church, Penelope had been convinced that Amy had something real, something she needed. Something her life had been missing. And she just hadn't realized what it was until Amy put a name on it: faith.

"Penelope, I'm so glad you're back and safe." Amy slid into the seat opposite Penelope.

"I'm glad, too. It was a real journey."

"You proved yourself, though, didn't you?" Amy turned her cup over for Becca to fill it. "Eggs and toast, Becca, the usual."

Amy pulled her red hair back in a ponytail and then she relaxed in the seat. She was waiting for details. Penelope realized that's what everyone would expect. But Amy was different. She had blue eyes that were wise and compassionate. She had strength—physical, mental and spiritual.

"I guess if I came here to prove that I could survive in the wilderness, I definitely did that. My brother will be proud that I can go without a department store." Penelope smiled as Becca returned, setting the plate with the cinnamon roll in front of her. The sweet, sticky mess, with lots of cinnamon, was exactly what she needed to get her day off to a good start. "I missed these."

"I bet you did." Amy sipped her coffee and then set the cup down. "People are talking. They say you went off in search of the treasure?"

Penelope swallowed a bite of cinnamon roll. "I did. I just thought, if I could find it, you would have the money you need to help the town, to help keep things going until the economy picks up."

Amy smiled, laced her fingers together and rested her hands on the table—and for a long moment she sat there. Penelope never expected tears. She grabbed a napkin and handed it to the other woman.

"I'm sorry, I don't mean to cry. But seriously, Penelope, there are so many people searching for this treasure, and it matters to me that you wanted it for us, for the town."

"I don't need the treasure, Amy."

"I know you don't. That doesn't always stop people."

"I know. But Amy, this town, the people here, you've all become so important to me."

"But how would you have found the treasure?"

Penelope looked out the window at a town wearing a thin coat of snow. She thought about Thanksgiving here, about the big community dinner. She thought about how they had all come together.

"Penelope?" Amy's voice was soft.

"I saw the map you were showing someone."

"Yeah, but seeing a map and then taking off on your own…"

"It was a crazy thing to do. But I have a photographic memory. I had taken a hike with one of the tours, and while we were walking, I thought I recognized something from the map."

"Photographic?"

Penelope nodded. "Please don't tell. It isn't a big deal. I just remember things that I see. I saw the map and I wanted to do something."

Amy reached for Penelope's hands. "You have my word. And while we're talking, I wanted to ask if you're staying."

"I plan on it. Why?"

"I wanted to ask if you'd help out with the Christmas pageant. We're having, well, fun. Life is a little crazy right now, with all of the new people in town, and the ladies…"

The unfinished sentence said a lot. Women from the city. And quite a few were like

Penelope; wealthy socialites looking for excitement. That had to be making life interesting for the locals.

"Sure, I'd be happy to help with the Christmas program," Penelope said. "I can decorate, or even help get the word out."

"You can sing." Amy waited until Becca refilled her cup and walked away. The waitress stood there for a moment longer than necessary. With a sweet smile from Amy, the girl rushed off.

Amy laughed a little. "That girl loves to hear what's going on. Anyway, I know you sing."

"I'm okay."

"I heard you sing in church. You're more than okay. We really need someone who can sing. Joleen, well, God bless her, she can't get the words right to 'Silent Night.' I don't know what it is about that song, but she constantly has angels appearing to the Wise Men and worse."

"Worse?"

"It's been a long week." Amy smiled. "So, what do you say?"

"I'll help. I'll do whatever you need."

Amy pulled her phone out of her pocket and frowned. Penelope waited, hoping the text wasn't bad news.

"Amy, are you okay?"

"Oh, yes, I'm fine. Penelope, Reed needs to talk to you. He wants me to walk you over to his office."

Chapter Nine

If he could have picked anywhere to be at that moment, Tucker wouldn't have picked sitting in Reed Truscott's office at seven in the morning. When Penelope walked through the door and saw him, that feeling doubled.

"Chief Truscott, how can I help you?" Penelope shoved her hands into her jacket pocket. Trembling hands, Tucker noticed.

He watched as she approached the desk. Man, he felt for her. He imagined himself standing in front of the principal's desk twenty years ago. She probably felt about the same way.

"Have a seat." Reed nodded toward an empty chair on the other side of his desk. "I just want to ask a few questions."

"Okay." She sat down but she didn't lean back. She didn't relax.

"Penelope, is there anyone you can think of who would be following you?" Reed could have done a better job of asking that question. Tucker wanted to retract it, to start with something that gave her the opportunity to think about what happened. Not that she really even knew. He had kept the footprints from her because he didn't wanted to scare her.

When he glanced her way she was staring at him. He smiled but she didn't return the gesture. Instead her gaze shot back to Amy, who had accompanied her.

"I can't think of anyone. It isn't as if I run with a rough crowd."

Reed smiled. He stretched and then he laced his fingers behind his head. "No, I didn't figure you were hanging with a dangerous crowd."

"So why would you even think that someone would be after me?" She scooted to the edge of her seat. "Why is Tucker here?"

She aimed the question at Tucker, not at Reed.

"I'm here because I went to Reed with some information."

"Information?" She remained on the edge of the standard office chair, jeans tucked into the snow boots she'd hiked out in. Her jacket wasn't the old down-filled coat she'd worn.

The brown coat was knee length and she pulled it close around herself.

"Penelope, there was someone at the cabin." Tucker scooted his chair so that he faced her. "I didn't want you to worry, so I didn't tell you that Clark and I found footprints and a campsite."

"You think it had to do with me."

"It happened the day after you showed up. I also think they followed us away from the cabin."

She shivered a little. "I can't imagine who it would have been."

Reed cleared his throat. "Could I add to this conversation? You are Penelope Lear."

"So?"

"Well, I think we have to consider the possibility that someone could take you for a ransom. This treasure map has brought people to town who aren't the most trustworthy. They want a treasure, and I don't think they care how they get it."

"But no one knew that I was going for a drive that day."

"No one?" Tucker found that hard to believe. He'd been around her and knew how she loved to talk.

She glanced at him. Or maybe it was more of a glare. An ice-cold, blue-eyed glare. "I bought a few supplies and rented a Jeep. I wanted it to be a surprise."

A smile tugged on the corners of his mouth, but he fought it back by clearing his throat. "Of course."

"Well, it obviously doesn't matter. If someone wanted to snatch me, they would have done it by now."

Reed returned to the conversation. Tucker watched the cop pull his gaze from Amy, back to Penelope. Four months changed things. It changed how people felt. It changed how Reed looked at Amy.

It hadn't changed Tucker much. He didn't feel as if he knew one thing more than when he'd left. Four months getting his head on straight should have done something more than have him thinking about Penelope Lear.

Last night he'd gone through his dad's paperwork. Of course he'd left everything to Tucker. Not that there was much of anything to leave. An old fishing boat, a truck and the house. He was still going through paperwork, but he didn't expect much more than that.

None of it really mattered. Saying goodbye would have mattered. He forced himself back into the conversation and listened as Reed explained to Penelope that she needed to stay close to town and not go off by herself. Tucker wondered how long she'd listen to the cop's advice.

The office door opened, bringing a gust of cold air and Herman Lear. Tucker glanced from the man in the doorway to the woman sitting a few feet away from him. She froze and then her mouth dropped a little. He hated what he saw. By calling her father, Reed had put her squarely back in Herman's control.

Obviously she thought he'd made the call, not Reed. She glared at him, her eyes tearing up for the first time since Reed had called her into his office. The idea of someone following her didn't upset her. Her father's presence did.

"What's going on?" Herman Lear stood in the center of the room, a dominating force in a black overcoat, his hair steel gray and his face weathered but still hard and unbending.

"Mr. Lear, I called you here because we have reason to believe your daughter's safety is in jeopardy."

"What makes you believe that?"

Tucker stood up and indicated for the older man to sit, mainly because they'd all relax if Mr. Lear wasn't looming over them. "Someone followed her into the woods."

"Do you have proof?"

"Someone was snooping around the cabin while she was there and someone followed us back to town."

Herman Lear turned his back on Tucker, ignoring the chair, and stared at his daughter. "Did you notice anyone?"

"Not once. It could be anything." Penelope's chin jutted and her voice was strong.

"I don't care. You're going to pack your bags and head home."

Penelope shook her head. "No, I'm not. I'm staying in Treasure Creek."

"I think this vacation of yours is over. I'm not going to leave you here and have something happen to you."

"Nothing is going to happen."

"Why in the world do you want to stay here?" Herman sat on the edge of Reed's desk.

"I love this town, Dad. And I don't think I'm in danger."

"Well, I think you are. I know you're an adult, but this is about your safety. We're flying out this afternoon."

"I'm not." She picked up her purse and stood. "Chief Truscott, I appreciate the warning. Dad, I'm not leaving."

She didn't tell Tucker goodbye, just glanced his way and then smiled at Amy as she walked out the door. Tucker watched as she walked across the snow-covered street in the direction of the general store.

Joleen Jones grabbed Penelope as she walked through the door of the general store. Penelope stiffened and then relaxed, because it was Joleen. Exuberant, energetic Joleen. Poor Mr. Peterson. It seemed that he was still the target of the socialite in the fur coat, suede boots and overdone jewelry. As horrendous as it all was, Joleen was still easy to like.

"Well, honey, it is about time you made it back to town."

Penelope smiled at the greeting. "It's good to be back."

She glanced in the direction of the police station and let out a quick sigh of relief because no one had followed her. So, now that she was here, what did she buy? How did she kill time in Treasure Creek's general store?

She could be like the men who stood on the corner with their cups of coffee. It wasn't good coffee. She'd tried it when she first came to town. And then she figured out that it was "guy" coffee. It was strong enough to cut through metal and was meant to keep women at bay.

The general store, she learned from Amy, was where the men of Treasure Creek came to hang out. Not to gossip, of course. Men don't gossip. They talk about the weather and about politics. And sometimes about what their neighbors were up to. But it was never gossip. Penelope smiled and then turned her attention back to the perfume cloud that was Joleen.

"Are you going to church tonight?" Joleen asked a little loudly. Probably more for Harry than Penelope.

"I might, if I can get away." From her parents.

But Joleen was going to church?

Penelope smiled, because she knew that people in town had prayed for Joleen. She was positive they'd prayed for her as well.

"Well, what about the Christmas pageant? My goodness, honey, you missed out on so much, and you weren't gone long at all. And not only that, but I heard you came back to town with that hunky lawyer who has been missing since June. Is he off his rocker?"

"What?"

Joleen softened her smile. "I mean, he took off on his own and he's been gone for months. That isn't something a sane person would do. People in town are talking, wondering if maybe he had some kind of breakdown."

"He seemed fine." Penelope sifted through the rack of jeans. Normal, plain old jeans. She pulled off a couple of pairs that would fit her and then grabbed a couple of sweatshirts.

"You're not going to wear that!?" Joleen covered her mouth with her hand and then turned a little pink because Harry cleared his throat. "Not that they aren't lovely."

"They're warm. If you ever end up lost in the woods, you'll appreciate warm. Hey, how is Delilah?"

"Who knows."

"I thought the two of you were friends."

"We were, until I realized she doesn't have a loyal bone in her body. And who needs friends who aren't loyal?"

Penelope nodded because she got that. Across the street at the police station, Tucker Lawson was telling people stories about her life. She supposed he thought he was protecting her, but he was really just signing his name on her fate. Her dad would claim her life for good, and all because Tucker came up with some crazy idea that people might follow her.

"I'm sure it's a misunderstanding." Penelope walked to the counter to pay for her items. The door opened and Delilah walked in. Joleen stalked out of the store.

Delilah, head down, walked to the back of the first aisle. Penelope smiled at Harry, his face red and his mouth in a grim line.

"It's always interesting." Penelope pulled out money for her purchases.

Harry glanced up and then back to his cash register. "I could do with a little less interesting, less excitement."

"Oh, come on, Harry, would you really want us all gone?" Penelope laughed because his face turned a deeper shade of pink. "Imagine life if we hadn't shown up."

"Yes, I imagine it quiet again."

"I know what you mean." But Harry was watching out the window. Joleen sashayed across the street to a small boutique that had probably never seen so much traffic.

Harry counted her change back and handed her the bag with the jeans and sweatshirts. "Those will do you a lot better the next time you're stranded in the cold."

Penelope managed to laugh. "I don't plan on letting that happen again."

Her mother was waiting on the sidewalk outside the general store. Penelope stopped, bags from the store hitched over her shoulder. Snow fell softly from the gray sky. A few people walked past them, pardoning themselves.

Victoria Lear looked perfect. She always looked perfect. Her hair, makeup, clothes, it was all part of the package. And Penelope had always felt a little like the discount kid.

Penelope had always been the one causing problems by chasing off after some new experience. Her mother had once told her that charity was about giving money, not about getting caught up in other people's problems.

"Your father told me we have a problem."

Penelope shrugged and started walking. Her mother walked next to her. "Mom, I'm not going home."

Victoria glanced at her, and then to her right. "I don't blame you."

"Excuse me?"

"I don't blame you. If you come home your father will take over. He doesn't mean to, but he does it. He can't help it. So you stay here and you find something that makes you happy."

"Is this a trap?" They were close to the little courtyard that would have been green and flowering if it had been summer. Instead it was covered in a dusting of fresh snow and sprinkled with lights that would sparkle this evening. Someone had built a snowman. He looked a little thin because the snow was scant and powdery.

"It isn't a trap. I want you safe. I also want you happy. That's what I noticed last night. I noticed that for the first time in years, even after everything you've gone through, you looked content."

"So you want me to stay?"

"Not forever." Her mom shivered. "Seriously, this is a place to visit, not a place to live. There's nowhere in this entire town to get a good manicure."

Penelope looked down at her hands, fortunately gloved and out of sight. "Thank you."

"You're welcome." Victoria kissed her cheek and Penelope breathed a deep sigh of relief. "I'm going back to our room. I think we'll leave tomorrow."

"I'll be back shortly. I want to peek in at the church to see if they've finished decorating."

"Penelope, please be cautious."

"I'll be cautious."

"And come home for Thanksgiving. It's a little over a week away."

Home for Thanksgiving. Earlier she'd been thinking of Thanksgiving in Treasure Creek, not at home in a formal dining room with a catered meal. Her thoughts were still on the holiday when she walked out of the church a few minutes later. Halfway down the sidewalk a hand touched her shoulder. Before she could scream, another covered her mouth.

Chapter Ten

Tucker clamped his hand over Penelope's mouth and waited for her eyes to connect with his before he moved his hand.

"An hour ago you were warned that you could be in danger, and now you're traipsing around town like you don't have a care in the world?"

Penelope's eyes narrowed. "I was with my mother, and it seems that the only thing I have to be afraid of is you."

Her heart still hammered her ribs, even though she knew she was safe, knew that it was Tucker and not some crazy person about to drag her away.

"I didn't want you to scream and cause heart attacks all over town. I saw you in the church and thought I'd invite you to lunch."

"Right." She walked down the sidewalk and he had to rush after her.

"I know you're upset, but you have to understand…"

"That you kept something from me and then, instead of telling me, you went to the local police. I understand completely. You thought I couldn't take care of this myself. I'm an adult. I'm obviously capable of taking care of myself. Did you know that I have been to Africa three times with a program that feeds orphans? I've been to South America two times to help build homes."

He opened his mouth, but what in the world was he supposed to say.

Perfect blond brows arched and she shot him a smug look before walking on.

"That's impressive." He finally got out the feeble compliment.

"It is, isn't it? My parents have always assumed I was in Europe or on a beach somewhere. Everyone thinks this is my big adventure. It isn't."

Even more impressive. And he'd labeled her as just another spoiled socialite who couldn't fight her way out of a wet paper bag. He'd fallen into the trap of stereotyping. The guy who hadn't judged his clients, the man who had believed in giving the benefit of the doubt.

He'd looked at her, at the whole package that was Penelope Lear, and he guessed who he thought she was. He'd been wrong.

Not that he hadn't been wrong before. He was starting to see that he wasn't a great judge of character. The experience with his mom should have proven that a dozen years ago, when he'd gone looking for her.

"I owe you an apology."

She stopped when she heard that and turned to smile at him. Man, she could be a flirt when the mood hit her. A cute smile, flashing blue eyes that sparkled with laughter, and a flip of blond hair over her shoulder. She nearly hooked him, the same way she'd hooked fish in the stream by the cabin.

Those poor fish probably saw her and jumped on the hook.

"You can buy me a real cup of coffee," she took a step back and tripped a little on an uneven brick. Tucker reached for her hand, remembering the ankle that had nearly kept her from making it back.

"I'll buy you coffee. How's your ankle?"

"Good today. It's wrapped tight, and the swelling has gone down."

"Glad to hear it."

"Because you don't want to have to carry me."

He couldn't have disagreed more. He

enjoyed carrying her. She was soft and light. It made him feel a little bit like a hero.

"If you needed to be carried…"

She coughed a little. "Please don't. I think this is getting a little too sweet. I like the Tucker who is a little dry, cynical and perturbed."

"I guess I'll have to find him."

"Much better." She slipped her hand into his for a second and then removed it. He glanced down to see if there was a reason why. She looked away. "I love the coffee at the diner."

"That's good." He reached for her arm, and she glanced down at his hand.

The diner was nearly deserted, but tables still covered with plates and half-empty glasses meant they'd barely missed the lunch crowd. No one greeted them.

"Let's sit by the window over there." Penelope limped a little as she crossed to a table in the corner.

He pulled out her chair and she sat down.

"Have you had lunch?" He picked up a menu with a list of sandwiches and desserts.

"No, but I'm all about a cup of coffee right now."

The waitress hurried over and he ordered two cups of coffee.

"So you're staying here?"

"I'm staying. What about you?"

"I'm going back to Seattle as soon as I get things settled."

She fiddled with her glass of water until the waitress walked away. When she looked up, Tucker was pretty close to thinking he should leave. He should have listened to his better sense, that told him to skip a cup of coffee with her. Especially after she told him about her trips to South America and Africa.

It was easy to think of her as an heiress, but when he started adding the layers it changed who she was.

"Is it that easy, Tucker? Do you just 'settle' losing your father the way you did." She looked up, blue eyes shimmering. "I mean, well, it can't be easy for you to walk away from here."

He wanted to whistle, because she had just jabbed something pretty sharp into his heart. And he'd really thought he was past feeling pain. Or at least more pain.

"There isn't anything for me here."

"No, of course not."

"What does that mean?" If she tried to tell him it didn't mean anything, he'd have to disagree. It was written all over her pretty, meddling face. She meant something by that comment.

"It means that I think you're still hurting. I'm not even sure if it is all about your dad. Something made you leave town. Something that pushed you to go off by yourself."

"I invited you to have a cup of coffee and I wanted to make sure you're okay. I didn't want to talk about my life, or what is going on with me."

"No, of course not."

She smiled, and for whatever reason, she dropped the subject.

Penelope watched emotion play across the features of the man sitting across from her. What had it been like for him, to come back to town after all of these months in the cabin? She thought it had to be a shock.

"Did you know that there have been several weddings and engagements since you left?" Penelope did a rapid change of subject, because the other felt off-limits, and she saw something in his eyes that looked broken.

"I had heard. Dr. Havens and his new nurse, Casey and Jake, the list goes on. Even Gage. That took my by surprise. I hope they'll all be very happy."

"Ahh, you believe that all marriages are doomed. You're probably especially predisposed to think that all of this romance is bunk."

"I'm busy, Penelope. Too busy for romance and too busy for games."

"Some marriages do last."

"I know they do, but surely you aren't optimistic about marriage, considering…"

She waited for him to finish and he didn't. She could fill in the blank, and she thought he could, too. Considering her parents' rather cool relationship, considering the fact that her dad had slipped into some nineteenth century idea of arranged marriages. Yeah, all things considered, she still wanted to be an optimist and believe in happily-ever-after.

But with someone who was there for her and present in the relationship. Not a detached businessman.

She looked at Tucker.

Or an overworked lawyer.

The big definite was that she wouldn't marry the type of man her father picked for her. That would mean marrying someone just like him.

"Yes, Tucker, I still believe in romance and real love. I believe in it, and I do know what my dad is doing."

"Oh."

"He wouldn't keep it a secret. He has even given me a list of options."

"Options, as in…"

"As in the men he considers suitable contenders. Don't worry, you're not on the list."

Did he look relieved? She thought he might. And then he looked toward the door. She glanced that way and saw a huge group of women about to enter.

"It's about to get very crowded in here." He pulled a few bills out of his wallet. "What do you say we hit the road."

"Afraid you'll be a target."

"You might think this is funny, but honestly, being in this town is a little uncomfortable. There's this woman named Delilah hanging around. She's pretty determined."

"She does come on rather strong." She took pity on him and stood. "Okay, you win, I'll let you escape."

"I'll walk you back to your B and B."

Sweet, and then it wasn't sweet. This was about the imaginary stalkers he thought were following her. *Thanks, but no thanks.*

"I don't need a babysitter. Seriously, what could happen to me in town?" *Or anywhere, for that matter.*

"I'm not doing this for that reason. I'm walking you back because it's what I want to do."

"That's nice." She shot him a teasing smile. "As a matter of fact, it's almost romantic."

"Don't make me reconsider."

The door opened and a cloud of perfume and cold air blasted into the diner. Tucker slipped an arm around her waist and eased her around the women and out the door.

It shouldn't have felt so good, that arm around her. But it did. It felt safe. It felt like the touch of someone she wanted in her life.

The thought of wanting Tucker in her life that way didn't make sense. She should be looking for someone safe, someone like that good-looking guide who had taken them hiking a couple of weeks ago. He seemed steady, dependable and like he wanted to spend time with a woman.

"Do you really plan on staying here?" Tucker asked the question as they walked through town toward the inn.

She drew her attention from the brick sidewalks and surrounding buildings. The gray sky was getting darker, a sign of dusk. Or a setting sun, if the sun had bothered to show itself, which it hadn't in several days. At least today it wasn't so cold that a person felt like their lungs would freeze if they took in a deep breath.

"I plan on staying for a while."

"You might meet someone, Penelope."

"Thanks for being so optimistic." She glanced up, smiling, and he laughed a little.

"I didn't mean it that way—I don't think."

"Right. How long are you staying?"

"Another week or two." He moved his hand from her back and shoved both his hands in his coat pockets. "I can't stay away from work for much longer."

"Why would you want to stay away?

His mouth tightened and his jaw clenched.

She'd guessed right. She also knew that he wasn't going to let her in. She didn't belong in the dark corners of his life where he kept his secrets.

"Penelope, you're determined, I give you credit for that." He stopped in front of the inn. The building was square, a little nondescript. She loved it, though. Her room was white, with big windows and down comforters and bedding. All white, sunny and clean. It was comfortably plain, without frills.

"Yes, I've always been determined. My dad acts as if that's a bad thing."

"I can imagine." He leaned and kissed her cheek. "Maybe I'll tell you someday. Not today."

"I know I'm pushy, but seriously, Tucker, if you need someone."

"Ditto. And since you're holding onto faith,

maybe say a prayer for me." He kissed her cheek again, a light gesture that couldn't mean more than friendship.

So why did her heart reach for his? Why did his request for prayer undo something inside her?

She reached for his hand and she didn't even know why. Maybe to keep him at her side a moment longer. Maybe to hold onto him until he shared something more meaningful than the weather?

His smile faded and he pulled loose. She let his hand slide from hers. He winked and walked away. She shivered a little and let out her breath as she whispered goodbye to his retreating back.

Time to let it all go and work on something that mattered. Amy had mentioned that Delilah was planning a trip to one of the native villages to deliver medical supplies and toys for the children. That was something worthwhile.

The ringing hammer signaled Jake's location. He was helping with preparations for the Christmas pageant. Jake? Christmas? Tucker shook his head at the strange turn of events. He did believe people could change, but seriously, in a matter of months this many changes was hard to digest.

Casey was with him. She twisted on the ladder and shot him a smile that wasn't exactly warm. He got it. He was the best friend who hadn't been here to interfere when their relationship started.

She didn't have to worry. He believed in live and let live.

"Tucker!" Jake put the hammer down and climbed down the ladder. "You here to help?"

"No, I don't think so." He didn't have a thing against the baby Jesus, but he didn't feel like celebrating Christmas or stepping back into this world.

He knew the Bible verses. He knew the songs. He knew the sermons. He knew so much, it was crammed into his mind and sometimes poked at him, like an old acquaintance trying to get his attention.

But his mom had ruined it for him. The woman who had read him the stories, taken him to church and sang the songs with him had stripped away his faith by walking out on her family.

When he walked back into this world he remembered too much.

"How does it feel to be back?" Jake stood

on the ground, slipped the hammer into the tool belt at his waist.

"I guess the answer you want is that it feels great." He touched the frame that he guessed might go to the nativity. Part of the stable. "The time out there was good for me."

"Yeah, I can see how it wouldn't be too bad to go off on a four-month hunting trip."

Tucker grinned. "Every man's dream, right?"

"Sure. If you can take the time off from work."

"I was covered."

To an extent. He called the office that morning and they were thrilled he'd been found. Not so thrilled with the four months he'd been gone. They wanted him back in a week. He thought it might take longer to get things settled. His dad's accounts, the boat, the house, none of it could be disposed of in a matter of days.

"How's the heiress?" Jake leaned to kiss Casey's cheek and she hurried away.

"Penelope is fine. Probably in more danger than she realizes, but her dad will take care of that."

"So, any change of heart on your part?"

"I'm not interested in her dad's offer. He

needs to let her find someone she loves, not someone he picks."

"That's usually the way of it. Love, I mean." Jake shot a glance over his shoulder to the other side of the room, where Casey was talking to a small group of people.

"Yeah, love." His friend was acting like a lovesick teen. It was a little annoying.

"Hey, did you know that Gordon is thinking of retiring. He's looking for someone he can trust to take over his practice."

Gordon Baker, one of the few lawyers in the area. Tucker smiled. "Nice, but I don't think I want to make that my career. Wills, divorces, land disputes. Isn't that about all he handles?"

"Not exciting enough for you?"

"I'm not going to lie and tell you that it sounds interesting."

"Your practice is so much better?" Jake handed him a hammer. "Here, help me get this board in place."

"I've built a name for myself in Seattle."

Jake pulled a nail out of his mouth. "Yeah, I know you have."

"You know, I've never wanted to hit you as bad as I do right now."

"Not true. You knocked me on my can when

we were juniors in high school. Remember, you liked Hannah Mahan."

"You took her to homecoming." He remembered and rubbed his knuckles that had been skinned in the altercation. "Yeah, I remember."

Jake laughed. "She married Ted Anderson, and they have six kids."

"That's pretty amazing."

"Yeah, but it doesn't have anything to do with you and Gordon's practice. I'm praying for you, Tucker."

"Good," he stepped back from the board. "I mean that. And now I'm going to take off. I have a lot to get done."

"Talk to Gordon."

"Probably not." Time for a change of topic. "What's going on with the treasure? Anyone found the location?"

"No. Amy has the real map, and I think Reed is keeping a pretty close watch on her, trying to keep her and the map safe."

"Yeah, I saw him keeping an eye on her today. The look I saw wasn't about a map."

They both laughed, and for a minute it felt like old times. Yeah, a person could go back. They couldn't get a life back, but they could go back and find things they'd misplaced.

Like friendships.

"Didn't Penelope go off looking for the treasure?" Jake pulled a few nails out of a nearby bag.

"Yeah, she did. Obviously, the only thing she found was a way to get lost and nearly get killed."

"She's under your skin a little, isn't she?" Jake pushed, as if pushing was a good idea. Tucker would have warned him, but Jake didn't seem to care.

"No, she isn't under my skin. She's a thorn in my side. She's a crazy female who doesn't know how to stay out of trouble."

"Yeah, that's what she is."

"I'm outta here." Tucker walked away and Jake was still laughing. Maybe it was about time to hit the road and come back to Treasure Creek when all of this nonsense faded. He could finish his dad's estate when women like Delilah, Joleen and Penelope got tired of playing in a small town.

He wished it was that easy.

He bumped into Reed Truscott when he left a few minutes later. The cop looked bristly and a little distracted.

"Reed, what's up?"

"Someone broke into Amy's place."

"Is she okay, and her kids?"

"Yeah, they're good. The map is gone. Someone saw a couple of men driving down the road."

Out of the corner of his eye, Tucker caught sight of someone heading in their direction. He glanced that way and realized it was Penelope. She hurried along, limping only a little. When she got closer, her smile faded.

"What's wrong?" She stopped next to Tucker and shot Reed a look. "Is Amy okay?"

"Amy's fine." Tucker explained. "The map is gone."

"Gone?"

"Stolen." Reed filled in the details and Tucker watched Penelope's eyes change. *Oh, great.* If he didn't know better, she was coming up with some kind of crazy plan.

And it wasn't his problem. He kind of liked that they were back in town and he could hand her off to the local police chief and her own father.

Chapter Eleven

Two days later, Penelope was in a Range Rover heading north. She was still thinking about the map and wondering who had taken it. At least she had freedom. Her parents left that morning for Anchorage. Yesterday Penelope had met with the Johnsons for a few hours before they left.

It felt good to have her life back, and that meant not having watchdogs. Even if it did sometimes feel like she was being watched. She ignored the feeling. She knew her dad and knew that he'd probably hired someone to watch her. She was more concerned with drawing a replica of Amy's map and figuring out who had taken it from her home.

For now, Delilah was sitting next to her in the back of the Range Rover and Penelope had given her bodyguard the slip. They were on their way to a village where a group from the community church planned to hand out toys and school supplies to the children, while Dr. Alex took care of medical needs.

They were a cute couple, Alex and Mary-ann. They had climbed aboard the truck that followed behind the Range Rover. The two were sitting in the front seat, side-by-side.

Penelope didn't feel at all jealous. Or that's what she kept telling herself. She wasn't jealous—not of Alex and Maryann. Instead, she felt a little empty. She wanted to know what it felt like, that kind of love that joined two people in a way that showed on their faces, in their eyes, the way they talked.

"Is Joleen in the other vehicle?" Delilah kept a steady gaze out the window when she asked the question.

"She isn't. She stayed behind. You know you should just be honest. Tell her you're not really interested in Harry."

"What if I am?" Delilah shot her a look and then turned back to the window.

"You're not. I heard you on the phone the other day. It wasn't Harry you were talking to."

Delilah shrugged and then she turned back around, smiling. "That was my best friend. We've known each other forever and always been there for one another. We have always said we'd marry each other if neither of us got married by the time we were thirty. And here we are, still single with the big birthday right around the corner. But honestly, he's not it for me. He's my best friend."

"I think friendship with the person you love would be the best way to start a marriage."

Delilah's laugh was loud. "You would think that."

"I've seen a lot of marriages that didn't include friendship."

"Why haven't you done something about that gorgeous he-man lawyer you spent the week in the woods with?"

"He isn't a friend. He thinks he has to take care of me. That isn't romantic."

"No, of course not." Delilah sighed. "I'm starting to think love and marriage aren't in God's plan for my life. I mean, the more I trust Him and try to have faith, the more it seems that everyone is finding love but me."

"Give it time and see what happens."

"This from the woman who has hooked the single most handsome man in town and doesn't know it. You don't even talk to him and he doesn't seem to care. I'm nicer than I've ever been, and no one wants to talk to me."

"Delilah, you're wonderful. You're beautiful

and fun. There are men who notice. You just have to give them time."

Delilah peered around the head of the driver in front of her. "There's the village. This is so exciting. I've never done anything like this."

Penelope remembered that feeling. She remembered the first time she landed in Africa. The first time she saw children waiting in line for food. These children weren't as destitute, but the needs were real. She remembered her heart filling up with love.

The village was small, with square buildings sided with plain wood siding. Smoke poured from chimneys. The main street through town bounced the Range Rover, as it hit potholes and bumps. Children ran out of a church building. The one thing that made it a church, that set it apart from the other buildings, was a simple cross next to the windowless door.

The vehicle stopped and Penelope reached for the door. She grabbed the box on the seat next to her as she climbed out. Cold air hit her, taking her breath. She shivered inside the heavy coat she'd bought at Harry's and hurried toward the church. Packed snow turned to ice made the going a little slick. She slid a little as she approached the door.

"Don't go down." Delilah shrieked from behind her.

"Thanks. Same to you." Penelope opened the door and hurried into the building, stomping her feet on the rug just inside the door.

Warm wood heat welcomed her. A grizzly bear of a man, with a heavy beard and a stocking cap pulled tight on his head, took the box from her. His brown eyes twinkled and a smile split the heavy whiskers.

"Welcome, my friends, I'm Pastor Johnny."

"Oh, well thank you for having us." Penelope pulled off her gloves and shoved them into her pocket. Children circled around her—tiny things with beautiful smiles and dark eyes. A few hugged her waist.

She couldn't imagine any love ever comparing to this. Her heart tightened and tears burned her eyes. She could do this forever. She could work in a mission somewhere. Maybe Delilah was right about giving up on marriage.

Behind her Delilah was talking to Pastor Johnny about the cold, about California and about the children. Penelope walked with the children to the front of the church. A piano sat in a corner. She pulled candy canes out of her pockets and handed them out. The children thanked her in bright little voices, their smiles widening.

"Do you want to sing a song?" It had been ages since she'd sat down at a piano, but she could manage a few songs. She opened the song book.

There was a rapid nodding of tiny heads, but their mouths were busy with candy. Penelope sat down at the piano and played "Silent Night." The children gathered close. Delilah walked down the aisle and joined her, singing words that weren't even close, and in a key that didn't exist. Penelope smiled at the other woman.

This was friendship. Penelope closed her eyes and played another song. "Away in a Manger." One of the children crawled onto the bench next to her.

"Will you sing with me?"

The little girl nodded.

"Okay, here we go. Everyone gather around and we'll sing a few songs before we go look at what is in those boxes."

"Shots." One little boy grimaced. "We don't want those."

"Oh, honey, the boxes don't have shots in them. Dr. Havens did bring medicine for you. You might have to get an immunization. But remember, it only stings for a second, but it keeps you from getting sick. And sometimes you could be sick for days. A little sting is better than that."

"Or going to the hospital like my brother had to do when he had pneumonia." A little girl with dark hair and clear blue eyes informed the group, in a voice that was mature beyond her years.

"Exactly." Penelope started with "Jesus Loves Me." The kids sang loudly.

When they finished, she played "Jesus Loves the Little Children." At the back of the church the door opened again, letting in a large crowd of people. She didn't look up. The children were singing softly, with sweet voices. If this kept them from thinking of immunizations, she was glad to help.

So this is where she slipped off to. Tucker stood at the back of the church and watched as Penelope Lear entertained a dozen children. It didn't even matter that Delilah was singing off-key next to her, throwing the whole thing off. As a matter of fact, Delilah's over-the-top singing almost made it more cheery.

"Coffee?" The man who had introduced himself as Pastor Johnny held a paper cup with steaming liquid.

Tucker took it. "Thanks."

He wasn't sure how cold it was outside, but he doubted the temperature registered above zero. He wasn't even taking off his coat yet. As good as the wood fire felt, it was going to take a while to thaw out after unloading a truck of supplies.

Penelope was singing another song, and all of a sudden, he found himself really wanting to believe again to have faith. Something about the song, and the way she sang it like she meant it, made him want to rethink his anger, to rethink his doubts. Why?

He watched her, an heiress who could have been soaking up the sun on a warm beach. Instead, she was playing the piano in a tiny church in an Alaskan village, surrounded by children who wanted to touch her and hug her. Man, he wanted to be one of those kids.

He was as enthralled with the silky, blond hair of hers as was the child who was running tiny fingers through the long strands.

Why? His mind took him back to that question. What was it about her that made him rethink everything? It had to be because she was here. The last place in the world that most women in her position would pick to spend their holidays, and she had picked it. She was here because of her love for people. She was here because of her faith.

"Tucker, could you help me set up the table for the immunizations?" asked Dr. Havens, a man who now had the look of a guy in love. His nurse and fiancé, Maryann, pretty and full of energy, was lugging boxes to a corner.

"Sure can." It wasn't why he'd come here. He'd followed the caravan out of town because when Penelope's dad left, he asked Tucker to keep an eye on her. They'd both known she'd give them the slip at the first opportunity.

She had tried.

He picked up one end of the folding table and Alex picked up the other. They carried it to a corner of the room and set it up. One of the other men carried a folding partition to enclose the little area.

"Anything else?" Tucker shoved his gloves in his coat pocket and pulled off his coat.

"You can help the others pass out the Christmas stockings that we brought." Maryann nodded in the direction of boxes that were being opened. "And we have boxes of food for Thanksgiving."

"I can do that."

The piano stopped playing. The children were moving away from it, and from the woman standing up, now that the music was over. She spotted him, freezing for a moment and then heading his way.

Her frown was a pretty obvious warning.

"What are you doing here?" She stopped in front of him.

"Same thing you are, helping."

"I don't believe that. I believe you're here to keep an eye on me."

"Right, that's what I do in my spare time. I follow heiresses who can't seem to stay out of trouble."

"I can stay out of trouble."

He couldn't stop the laughter. "For how long. Give me an amount of time you can go without getting yourself into some kind of scrape."

"That's mean." She walked away and he followed.

"I'm sorry."

She turned and walked backward, nearly tripping over a box. He grabbed her hand and pulled her away from it. She glanced back and lost her balance. Her grip on his hand tightened and they both laughed.

"I can stay out of trouble for at least five minutes." She admitted with a sweet smile.

"Your dad did ask me to keep an eye on you." The truth slipped out and he watched her smile fade.

"Thanks. And here I thought we were

actually friends. Instead, you're just another person assigned to keep me out of trouble."

"I don't do your father's bidding, Penelope. I am your friend, that's why I told you the truth. I'm here because I'm your friend, not because your dad asked me to be here."

Her eyes widened and her mouth parted. She was as shocked by that as he was.

He hadn't planned on friendship with her. He had planned to get her back to town and be done with the little nuisance. Instead, here he was. He was out in the freezing cold because she couldn't stay in town and out of trouble.

Instead, she stood in front of him in jeans, a sweatshirt from Harry's and insulated boots.

"We need to get busy." She touched his arm and walked away, joining Delilah, Maryann and others who were busy pulling stockings from boxes.

Tucker watched and then he went in search of something else to do, something that would give him a few minutes to get his good sense back.

Tucker caught up with her as everyone was getting ready to head back to town. "Ride back to town with me?"

Delilah slipped away and left Penelope to

face Tucker. He took the box she held and left her with nothing to do but stare at him. She pushed her hands into her pockets and just stood there like some silly, addled schoolgirl who didn't know what to do when the captain of the football team carried her books.

Not that she'd ever been to a school where there was a captain of a football team. She'd gone to private schools, and none had been big on sports.

But that was her mind wandering. She blinked and refocused on the man in front of her, and he was anything but a lanky teen. He was definitely a grown man, with grown man shoulders and a grown man voice that was husky and strong.

"I have a ride. I came with a group from the church."

"I'm aware of that."

"So why are you asking me to ride back with you?" She thought she knew why, but she wanted something else from him, some other reason.

Expecting him to say he wanted to spend time with her was ridiculous. He was taking over for her father.

"We both know why I'm asking you to ride with me. It would make everyone feel a little better if you were with me."

"It would make my dad and the police chief feel better if I rode with you."

"Exactly. Do you have everything you need?"

"Of course. Let me tell Delilah that I won't be riding back with her."

"I'll walk over there with you."

She muttered under her breath but didn't bother arguing with him. She'd been dealing with men like him her entire life. He was just another alpha male in her world. What she wouldn't give for a nice, friendly beta male. She wanted a guy who would take off his tie in the evening and go for a walk. A man who didn't leave a birthday party to rush off to the office where some important paper couldn't wait until the next day for his signature.

A hand touched her back. "I'm sorry."

She turned, not expecting the soft smile on his face or the way he stepped a little closer.

"It isn't your fault," she said.

"I guess it isn't, but still, I know this isn't easy."

"It isn't." She pulled her coat off the hook by the door and stepped aside to pull it on as a few people walked out, letting a blast of frigid air into the building. She shivered as she pulled on her coat. "I'd almost prefer being back in the cabin."

She thought about the cabin a lot in the last few days. She thought about the Johnsons, who had just arrived in Treasure Creek the day before, but had headed south to visit relatives for the holidays. She thought about the fireplace and the aroma of popcorn they'd popped over the fire.

Unfortunately, her memories of the cabin also included the man standing in front of her. He reached for her coat and helped her slide her left arm into it, and then he paused in front of her. She froze when he reached for the top button of her coat and fastened it. She covered his fingers with her own and stepped away from him.

"I can do it." Her fingers trembled and she couldn't look up. It was good to have something like the buttons to concentrate on.

"I'm sorry." He backed away, forcing her to look at him. "I'm going to make sure the truck is getting warm."

"I'll be out in a minute."

A few minutes later a horn honked outside the door. Penelope waved goodbye to Pastor Johnny and hurried out the door. Tucker's truck was parked a short distance from the door. The passenger side door opened a few inches, pushed from the inside.

She reached for it and then paused—because,

what if it wasn't Tucker. What if someone really did want to abduct her? She'd gone through her entire life keeping those threats pushed to the back of her mind, never really thinking about them. But the last week had changed her ability to ignore the possibility.

She peeked into the truck. Tucker smiled and held out a hand.

"Need a lift?"

She ignored his hand and grabbed the handle on the inside of the door. She pulled herself up into the mammoth vehicle and sank into heated leather seats. "Feels great in here."

"Yeah, a lot better than walking."

"Much better. But it really wasn't so bad."

"You were tough on the trail, Penelope."

"Thanks."

And then they didn't talk for a long time. It was dark and the headlights shone on the snow-covered roadway. It wasn't even dinnertime yet. She watched out the side window, thinking about all of the places she could have been.

Would she trade this place, this moment, for those other places? She didn't think so. She had just witnessed the joy of receiving on the faces of dozens of young children. Nothing could compare to sharing that experience.

"That's a pretty serious look."

She turned to face Tucker. He glanced her way and then back to the road in front of them.

"You're supposed to watch the road, not me."

"I thought you might be asleep."

"No, just thinking about how great that was back there."

"Yeah, it was good."

"You sound so detached. Don't tell me your heart is two sizes too small."

He laughed a little. "Maybe it is. I think I might have dropped a couple of sizes this summer."

"What happened?"

He shrugged and kept driving, both hands on the wheel.

"I'm not sure what you mean."

"That's always your answer, and I don't believe that nothing happened. I don't believe you took off into the woods for a few months just because it felt like the thing to do. I think something happened."

"Like my dad dying before I could get home."

"Keep going."

He shot her another look and shook his

head. "Let's just get back to Treasure Creek. I'll even buy you a nice dinner."

"Do you ever talk to anyone about the things that bother you or do you hold it all inside?"

"I hold it inside. It's what I'm comfortable with."

"Yeah, you look comfortable."

"My dad could have been saved with a bone marrow transplant. He never told me I might have been able to save his life."

She leaned back in the seat and stared straight ahead, trying to process what he'd shared with her. It hurt her to think about something so devastating to a person's life. It was his life. She didn't know how he could get up each day, let alone face his life.

"I'm sorry."

"You don't have to be sorry, Penelope."

She nodded. Yes, she did. She'd pushed him until he'd given in and shared. Now that she had the information, she was sorry she'd made him tell.

Tucker slid his hand across the seat and reached for Penelope's hand. She touched his fingers and then clasped his hand in hers.

"I'd head for the mountains, too." She finally spoke, her voice soft and wobbly. He knew that tears would be trickling down her cheeks.

"Yeah, it was a rough summer." He slowed for his next turn, hitting his turn signal and easing onto the brakes. "After the funeral I got a phone call from Seattle."

"What happened in Seattle?"

He made his turn. "I got a client freed from jail after a pretty serious DWI charge."

"Okay. I'm sure lawyers do that every day."

"To repay my faith in him, he waited a few weeks, got drunk and drove into a car driven by a seventeen-year-old girl. She died at the scene. He lived."

He was still angry. It hit him full force, the way it always hit him. Every time he thought about that girl losing her life, when he thought about the Johnsons not making it home in time to tell their son goodbye, and when he thought about his dad dying without him, it hurt. It made him want to go track that drunk driver down. It made him think about everything he wished he would have said to his dad—the good things, not the negative.

"Have you talked to her parents?"

That was the last thing he expected Penelope to ask. He swung his gaze in her direction, but he didn't trust this road at night, not enough to give her a long look.

"You're kidding, right?"

"No, I'm not. I think you need to forgive yourself. Some horrible things happened to you and you're acting as if you did it all. You didn't know about your dad, so how could you have saved him? You didn't know that man would drink and drive that again."

"I should have called my dad more often. I should have let that drunk be found guilty."

"But you couldn't have known."

"No, I couldn't have known."

"And you've tried to handle it all alone."

Great, she's going to keep pushing. Why did women always want to fix him? He had always kind of liked his angry, detached persona. He didn't owe anyone anything.

"I'm fine on my own, Penelope. I've handled life for a long time that way."

"Yes, and you've done a great job."

"You want me to pray and have faith, don't you?"

"I'm not going to push that on you. I found answers in faith. I'm not going to tell you that faith or God are the answer for *your* life."

"But…"

She laughed a little. He'd missed that laugh.

"But maybe, if you'd give God a chance…"

"Right."

"Maybe cut yourself some slack. You might call those parents. Maybe if you—"

He had to cut her off. "I'm not going to soothe my conscience at their expense. They lost their daughter. They don't need to hear from the lawyer who helped set that monster free."

"Maybe."

If they weren't in the truck and if he hadn't been driving, he might have kissed her. It seemed like the perfect way to stop her from pushing further. It seemed like the perfect idea, no matter what.

Chapter Twelve

They parked next to Penelope's bed-and-breakfast, also a short walk from the church. She glanced in the direction of the pretty little building. It looked so quaint among the town's other buildings. Streetlights glowed, casting circles of light on snow-covered walks. A few shop windows were decorated with Thanksgiving cut-outs, turkeys and pilgrims made out of plastic.

"Do you want to have a cup of coffee?" She held onto Tucker's hand as he walked her up the sidewalk.

He glanced from her to the church. "I can't. I need to think about some things."

"I'm sorry for being so hard on you."

He smiled, towering over her with broad shoulders that were even broader in the heavy coat. A stocking cap covered his head. He touched her cheek with a gloved hand. "You pushed me to think about things that I've dwelt on but haven't dealt with. Thank you."

He kissed her softly, tenderly, his lips moving over hers and holding her captive. She held onto his arms, holding onto the last bit of sanity she thought she possessed. In his arms she was strong. She wasn't Penelope Lear. She was someone who knew how to survive. In his arms, she didn't back down.

She kissed him back. He murmured that she was beautiful as he kissed her cheek and stepped back.

"I'll talk to you tomorrow." He winked and walked away. The Alaska cold had never been as frigid as it was at that moment, when his warmth evaporated and she stood alone on that sidewalk in the dark. His back was a silhouette framed by the halo of a streetlight.

She watched him change directions and walk toward the most unexpected building, the church. He opened the door and a shaft of golden light hit the white ground outside. And then the door closed. She prayed he'd find what he was looking for inside.

The door behind her opened. She turned and smiled at Joleen.

"Hey, sweetie, want to grab a bite to eat?" Joleen was still wearing fur. She hadn't quite bought into wearing what the locals wore. She said she just couldn't do it, not even if it won Harry Peters's heart.

"I'd love to."

"Was that the handsome lawyer-turned-recluse out here with you?"

Penelope glanced toward the church and nodded. "It was."

Joleen whistled. "Honey, I've seen some handsome men in my time, but that one is a keeper."

"Not really." Penelope smiled at Joleen. "How are things going with you and Harry?"

"I don't think he's interested at all. If he is, well, that Delilah will get him. He's her Samson. I think she wants him to spite me."

"She doesn't, but that's for the two of you to work out. Just talk to her."

"I don't know if I want to. But he's a sweet man, that Harry is. He's just real, you know what I mean?"

"Yes, I think I do."

It was wrong for her to think about Tucker. Every detail about a man, every character trait shouldn't make her think of him, wonder about him, or want to talk to him. She'd never had a relationship with a man that included wanting to just be around him.

She wished Wilma Johnson was still in town so they could talk about it.

"Stop looking so glum, sweetie. It'll all work out. You'll see. I'm learning a lot in this little ol' town. And one thing I'm realizing is that God has a way of working things out."

"Thanks, Joleen, I appreciate that."

They walked into Lizbet's and sat down at a corner table. The place was pretty quiet. A few couples sat together at one large table. A couple of men sat in a corner booth. They turned to stare when Joleen and Penelope entered. Penelope shivered and it wasn't from the cold. She couldn't take her eyes off two men in flannel jackets, caps pulled low over shaggy heads.

"That's a couple of hoodlums if ever I did see a couple." Joleen slid her coffee cup to the side, and when the waitress approached, she asked for just a glass of water with a slice of lime.

The waitress shook her head. "Joleen, you try that all the time and you know we don't have limes."

"Sorry, honey. How about water on the rocks with a squeeze of lemon juice."

"You got it."

The waitress took their order and hurried away.

"I don't feel real comfortable in here right

now." Joleen shot a look in the direction of the men at the corner table. "What do you say we get our food to go?"

Penelope watched the men, and the fear that had been an ember started to grow. She nodded. "Yes, I think leaving would be a good idea."

One of the men folded a piece of paper and slipped it in his pocket. He continued to watch her, and she stared back until she lost her nerve. His eyes were narrow and cold. She shivered and looked away.

At least the two of them were together, she and Joleen. But it made her mad that she had to be afraid. She wouldn't have been thinking like this if Tucker hadn't put the thought in her mind.

Tucker opened his door the next morning to find his friend Jake standing outside.

"What are you doing here so early?"

"Thought you might have a cup of coffee to share with a friend." Jake shrugged out of his coat and hung it on the hook next to the front door.

"Yeah, right. I do have coffee, but I can tell by the look on your face that you have a lot more on your mind than that."

Tucker motioned in the direction of the

kitchen and Jake led the way, leaving a trail of melting snow in his wake. Tucker walked into the kitchen behind him and Jake was already getting a cup out of the cabinet.

"Sure, help yourself."

Jake grinned. "Want me to pour you a cup?"

"Since you're already there, yeah, sure."

Tucker sat down at the kitchen table and waited. He gave up being patient when Jake sat down, stirred sugar into his cup and started to drink his coffee.

"Why are you really here?"

Tucker didn't want coffee. He'd had nearly a pot since he got up that morning.

"Heard you made an appointment to talk to Gordon Baker."

Tucker had started to pick up the cup, but he set it back down. "There's nothing secret in this town, is there?"

Jake laughed. "Not at all. I also heard you were seen kissing Penelope Lear."

"Nice, now you're gossiping."

"Not so. If it's the truth, it isn't gossip. Is it true?"

"It's true."

"Penelope Lear and talking to Gordon. Interesting."

Tucker sighed. "Jake, I really don't want to talk about this."

"Of course not. So let's move on to something else. I'd like for you to be my best man."

"If I can't talk you out of it, I guess I'll walk you to your fate."

Jake grinned. "Don't worry, you'll get your turn."

"I don't plan on it."

"The second bit of gossip is that you left Penelope Lear and headed for church."

"Man, this is about to do me in. Why in the world would I want to stay in a town that has spies on every corner?"

"Because it's a great place to be." Jake got up to refill his cup. "Because living here changes a man. It settles you. Everything isn't a rush, another case, another deal."

"Family values and happily-ever-afters."

"Sarcasm and chronic indigestion is so much better." Jake sat back down. "Oh, sorry, did you want more coffee?"

"I've had enough." He'd had more than enough.

"Yeah, but I'm not done. I'm here to see if you need to talk to a friend. Yeah, I know that church is a great place to unload some troubles, but I thought—"

"That I'd share so you could go back and report what you learned."

Jake had the good sense to look a little sorry. "Whatever you tell me is between us."

"Yeah, I know that. I'm just a little tired of my life being up for debate. Gage was here last night quizzing me. I'm thankful for friends, but sometimes space is good."

"Right. I'm sorry about that." Jake sat back in the chair. "Are you getting things wrapped up here?"

Tucker was able to smile. "My dad was a pretty savvy investor. I've found things I hadn't expected."

"Yeah, I kind of figured that. He would share from time to time."

He hadn't shared with Tucker. "I should have called him more often."

"You didn't know."

"That isn't an excuse. Man, Jake, I didn't get to tell him goodbye. Every single day I wake up thinking about that and wondering if he knew that I loved him. But we were so busy being men, we couldn't let go of our stubbornness."

"Men do that sometimes." Jake didn't smile. "Look at my struggles with my own kid. She had me pretty twisted up with worry, but she's doing great now. We're both doing great. We stopped being angry and we—" he cleared his throat "—we realized it was okay to be loved."

"I'm glad you've found that." Tucker leaned his chair back and thought about the changes in his friend. It wasn't all bad, a family coming together, finding some happiness.

Tucker's dad had been his hero—and they'd fought like crazy.

"What about you?"

Tucker set the chair back down on all four legs. "I'm going to be okay. I called Anna's family last night. I explained who I was. I don't know why I called. I'm not sure if they had ever given me a thought, but I needed to tell them how sorry I am."

"Did it help?"

"Yeah, it did. I also decided to take a big chunk of Dad's savings and start a scholarship for children who have lost a parent to a drunk driver."

"That's pretty great, Tucker. Let me know if I can help."

"I will."

Jake glanced at his watch. "I have two ladies waiting for me to take them shopping. Are you going to be at the practice tonight?"

"Practice?"

"For the Christmas pageant. I'm sure we could use your bass voice."

"I don't think I'm up for that. It's been a long time since I've sang." Especially in church.

"Yeah, well, we could use you if you decide to show up. Don't worry, I'll protect you from the swarms of single women who are going to flock you. Dressed like that, they probably think you're one of the locals and not one of the burnt-out businessmen types that they're trying to escape from."

"I'll wear a suit and tie."

"Right, throw 'em off the scent."

Tucker walked Jake to the front door. His truck was idling in the driveway.

"Give Penelope my regards." Jake laughed as he walked away.

"Don't slip on the ice and break your stinking neck." Tucker walked back inside, but he couldn't get his mind back on the work he needed to do. Instead, he pulled out pictures of his dad, of the two of them.

And his mind kept returning to Penelope. He was staying far away from that pageant practice.

The room grew crowded as people gathered for the Christmas pageant practice. It was almost too warm with so many people. Penelope pulled off her coat and carried it under her arm. As she glanced around she smiled. She was starting to look like a local. In her boot-cut jeans, sweatshirt and insulated boots, she fit in. She loved fitting in.

Joleen moved through the crowd wearing her heavy faux fur coat and cap. And Joleen fit in, in her own special way. She probably looked just as out of place in her small Tennessee town as she did here.

She was just her own person.

Which was what Penelope was becoming.

People started to group up. Penelope hadn't been to a practice before. At first she'd been new to town and hadn't felt like she should. Then she had taken her little trip into the woods. She refused to call it "getting lost."

Today Amy had invited her to join them. It had been another step in becoming a part of Treasure Creek. She'd even looked at a little house on the edge of town.

She had driven past Tucker's dad's house and watched Tucker loading a few things in the back of his truck. He probably wouldn't be here long. She told herself it didn't matter. He wasn't the reason she was staying here. She was staying because she wanted to be from Treasure Creek.

It was no longer about finding someone to spend her life with. She wasn't worried about her dad trying to pick a husband for her. She'd refuse. She was almost twenty-seven, and she wasn't going to allow her life to be arranged that way.

Why in the world had it taken her so many years to realize she didn't have to hide who she was or what she wanted?

She moved to a corner and watched the crowds of people. She watched Joleen turn away from Harry, like she hadn't seen that he was heading her way. *Oh, big mistake.*

As soon as she could get Joleen alone, she'd try to help her. Poor Joleen, she was either coming on too strong or making poor Harry think she didn't like him at all.

"What are you doing over here in the corner? Don't tell me you're a wallflower?" The husky voice was familiar and set a shiver loose down her spine.

She smiled up at Tucker. He was wearing a heavy, flannel shirt and jeans. Every single woman in the place appeared to be eyeing him.

"I am a wallflower. It's easier to watch people from the sidelines. And you're trying to blend in, but instead you've made yourself a target for every single woman on the hunt for a rugged bachelor from Treasure Creek."

"Which is why I'm hanging with you tonight. It's simple. I stick close to you and they all think I'm taken."

"But you're not." Her heart *ka-thumped* in a funny way.

"No, I'm not."

"What if I want to talk to a man tonight? Someone other than a confirmed bachelor pretending he's not a lawyer?"

"Do you?"

Her heart beat a little harder and she didn't want to play his games. She stared into eyes that changed colors depending on the lighting and what he wore. But they were always warm, always so alive in a face that had become familiar and a part of her dreams.

"Maybe." She looked away because it hurt too much. Her heart hurt.

"I won't get in your way." He smiled and then winked. "I'll even go stand in a corner by myself if you want."

Did she want him gone? Did she want to feel that cold again, the cold she'd felt the other day when he walked away after kissing her? She didn't think so. She wanted to feel warm and safe.

He was anything but safe.

"You can stay."

"Thank you." He moved a little closer to her side. "I saw you drive by today."

"I was looking at a house that I might buy."

"You're thinking of staying here?"

"I know that's hard for you to imagine. I saw you packing and I know you can't wait to get back to your life and career. But I love it here. I love that life is slower paced and people know one another."

"They know each other in the city."

"I know, but it isn't that. It's…it's just that this is the type of place I've always wanted to be from."

"It's a fantasy, Penelope. This isn't a perfect place with perfect people."

"I'm aware of that. I know life won't be perfect here. But when it isn't perfect, I'll have friends who actually care enough to listen to me, or to give me advice."

"Not many of those people in your life back in Anchorage?"

"Not really."

"Yeah, I guess you have a point. People here care enough to get involved. You'll fit in. You like to involve yourself in other people's lives."

She looked up, unsure of what to say to that comment.

"I mean that in a good way," he explained. "I called Anna's parents. I needed to tell them how sorry I am."

"How did they take it?"

He glanced away, but not before she saw the raw pain in his eyes. "They didn't blame me as much as I blamed myself."

"I'm glad you called them."

He only nodded. Someone started to play the piano. Penelope glanced that way. It was time for her to sing.

"Are you going to sing?"

Tucker shook his head. "Not me, but thanks for asking. You go ahead. I'll be here when you get done. I'll walk you back to your lodging."

"I don't need a bodyguard."

He touched her cheek, surprising her. "I'm a friend, not a bodyguard."

She nodded and hurried away. But she couldn't escape how it felt when Tucker touched her that way. She couldn't run from what she knew about herself and the way he would break her heart.

Chapter Thirteen

If he'd planned the last three weeks of his life, Tucker wouldn't have planned Penelope Lear. Last spring, when her dad contacted him, he'd made it clear she was the last thing he wanted. Herman Lear had laid it all out: the daughter who was putting herself in danger by taking off to parts unknown and telling her family she was on the beach at some exclusive resort; the need to have her in a secure relationship to keep her safe; and the idea that the man needed to be as strong-willed as Penelope.

Tucker had said a happy "no thanks." Herman had asked him to travel to Anchorage for a few meetings, chance meetings with Penelope. Again, Tucker had declined. He hadn't wanted a socialite with more will than sense.

He shook his head as he watched her cross

the room and take her place with the crowd that gathered to sing. She was more a part of Treasure Creek than a part of the other crowd of women who had showed up in town. She had managed to reinvent herself. Or maybe not.

Without thinking it through, he started across the room, drawing closer to the choir. Maybe she hadn't reinvented herself, rather she'd found herself.

That didn't make him feel any better. It only complicated things. She was unexpected. She was a mystery. Man, she was under his skin. Jake had been right about that. She was under his skin to such a degree, he was actually talking to Gordon Baker about taking over his law office in Treasure Creek.

What kind of fool did that? Traded a six-figure income for something that would be comfortable, but little more?

The same kind of guy that was thinking about coming clean with Penelope Lear. She had a right to know that he'd been on the short list of potential husbands.

He didn't want to think about her reaction when he told her.

The choir started to sing. Jake motioned him forward. Right, they needed a bass. He shook his head. Jake nodded toward the group of people singing. That's when Penelope caught his eye. She smiled. That's all it took for him to lose it.

The women parted, leaving a space next to Penelope. He stepped onto the stage and slid in next to her. He refused to look at Jake. *Some friend.*

The woman on his right pushed a little, edging him closer to Penelope. Voices rose together, but definitely not in unison. "Silent Night"? He wished. If he blocked it out, he was sure he heard dogs howling in the distance. It sounded more like a round—like "Row, Row the Boat."

Someone wasn't even singing the right words. He glanced to the left and made eye contact with Harry Peters, who happened to be standing next to the offending soprano—Joleen. Or that's what he thought her name was. Eyes closed, she tilted her head up and belted out the lyrics that didn't match anything he'd ever heard. Harry was grinning.

"Be nice." Penelope leaned toward him and whispered.

"I'm good." He cleared his throat and joined the choir.

Penelope was laughing just a little. With her eyes closed, she looked perfectly innocent. He wanted to hug her tight.

For some reason, the choir shifted from "Silent Night" to "Amazing Grace." It was a modern version that he'd never heard and he didn't know the words. Neither did Joleen, but this time she stopped singing. He appreciated that she knew when to let it go.

He glanced her way and Joleen was staring at the star on the opposite side of the room. She raised her hand to brush at her cheeks. People had a lot more layers than he'd ever given them credit for.

The song continued with the words "my chains are gone." Tucker took a deep breath and couldn't stop himself from looking down at his hands. Chains. They'd been wrapped around his heart for a lot of years, tying him to the past, to his mother's walking away, to lost faith.

"I have to go," he whispered in Penelope's ear and then he moved back, moved away from the group and away from the words of that song.

"Tucker?" She reached for his hand and he shook his head. "Can I help?"

He shook his head but he didn't turn to look back at her. Her eyes would be wet with tears. She'd have that look on her face, like he was some lost animal she needed to rescue from a shelter. He didn't need that.

He didn't need Jake to follow him, or the pastor of the church. He left the building as Amy discussed the Christmas pageant and how life had changed for all of them in the last year. But God's love was unchanging.

For the first time he was really thankful for the cold air that hit full force as he walked across the street to his parked car. The streets were empty. Everyone was inside practicing for the pageant, or at home where a sane person should be.

Someone rounded the corner of the B and B.

Tucker walked in that direction, because who in their right mind would be walking around at this time of night and in this cold? Someone like him, who'd had enough of Christmas in November, enough of the hopeful optimism that clung to this town like the icicles that hung from the buildings.

But a man lurking behind a building didn't seem like the normal MO of a person trying to escape Christmas cheer.

Jake had called today to tell him more about this map situation. People were getting a little crazed. If it wasn't women looking for single men, it was single men looking for hidden treasure.

Maybe all of these people should head back to wherever they came from and try finding some reality. He might just take his own advice. He would take it, as soon as things were settled. As soon as the song the choir had been singing stopped going through his mind in a continuous loop.

The man he'd seen came around the far corner of the B and B and headed down the street. Tucker jumped in his car and followed. By the time he got down the side street, the guy was gone.

He told himself it had been nothing. He told himself that it had nothing to do with Penelope. That was probably the case, but the memory of unexplained footprints in the snow was a hard thing to forget.

It was hard to forget, or pretend, that it had nothing to do with Penelope Lear.

Practice ended with a loud version of "Joy to the World." Penelope headed for the coat rack by the back door. She didn't make it. Joleen headed her off at the pass, her smile big.

"Where'd that gorgeous lawyer go?"

Penelope moved past the other woman and reached for her coat. "I don't really know."

"Are you going to let him get away?"

"I'm not going to chase after him." She was immediately sorry for the hasty words. Joleen bit down on her bottom lip and looked back to the spot where Harry Peters was taking to Amy.

He glanced their way and turned a little red.

"I'm scaring the daylights out of that man."

Penelope hugged her new friend. "Maybe a little. I'm new to this faith business, Joleen, but I really believe God has a plan, and I think you don't have to push so hard. Maybe just be Harry's friend."

Delilah approached cautiously, stopping a short distance away from them. "I was going to get a cup of coffee at the diner."

Penelope nudged Joleen. "I'm going to my room. I bet Joleen would love a cup of coffee."

Delilah sighed a little. "Joleen?"

"I'd love coffee."

Penelope nearly clapped. That was one problem solved. And if Joleen settled down and backed off, maybe she'd have a chance with Harry. The two women talked as they put on coats and boots.

Penelope walked away. Coffee didn't even sound good. Figuring out Tucker Lawson, that's what she really wanted to do.

As much as she wanted to put him in a suit

and tie and send him back where she thought he belonged, there was something about him, something sweet and endearing. She sighed and walked out the door.

A truck pulled in front of her before she could cross the street. She jumped back a little, chiding herself for her rapidly beating heart. Between her dad and Tucker, she was jumping at every shadow.

The window of the truck rolled down. Tucker leaned out. "Get in and I'll give you a ride."

"It's a two-minute walk."

"I know, and it's a walk I don't think you should take tonight."

She wanted to walk, she wanted to clear her mind, she wanted to pray. She wanted to find peace, because it was just five weeks from Christmas, and this Christmas would be different for her. This year she would face it as a believer, someone with a vested interest in the life of the baby born in that manger. That baby had a vested interest in her life.

"Penelope, I know you love to argue, but if you could just get in the truck and argue later."

"Fine." She walked around the front of the truck and climbed onto the passenger seat. Tucker shifted into first gear and pulled away from the building just as Amy James walked out with Reed Truscott. Interesting.

Penelope glanced back, wondering if maybe there could be something between the two. But wouldn't that be almost the same as an arranged marriage? The type of marriage her own father wanted for her? Amy should find someone she loved, in her own time and in her own way. She shouldn't marry too quickly because it was what her husband asked her to do.

Reed was handsome and obviously cared about her. That didn't make him the right choice.

"Sudden interest in Amy and Reed?" Tucker slowed near the B and B but he didn't stop.

"Where are we going?"

"For a little drive. I will take you home, but I wanted a few minutes to talk, without someone walking up to us, asking questions or giving us that look, as if we're the next couple to fall."

"That obviously isn't going to happen." She didn't think it would happen. But her heart fluttered a little at the thought of it, at what it would feel like to be loved by a man who was strong, intelligent and someone different than anyone she'd ever known.

"No, that probably isn't going to happen," Tucker echoed, his voice soft.

He parked off a side street, and from that distance the town looked like a miniature Christmas village. She wanted to box it up and take it home with her, along with all of the feelings of being a part of something wonderful. She wanted to keep this in her heart forever.

"What's up?" She pulled off her gloves and unbuttoned the top button of her coat. The heater of the truck was blowing hard, and she didn't have a chilled bone in her body.

Tucker shrugged and she knew this moment would change everything. He was staring straight ahead, his profile handsome but unsmiling. She reached for his hand and waited, her breath held.

She imagined several things. She thought he might be about to tell her that he was going home, back to Seattle. She had expected that, so the words wouldn't take her by surprise. She'd expected him to leave sooner, really. Or maybe he would tell her that she should go back to Anchorage, back where she belonged. People did like to tell her what they thought was best for her.

He turned, his smile softened by the day's growth of sandy brown whiskers. He held her hand, raising it to kiss her palm. She didn't want him to stop there. She wanted to be held close, against a solid chest that made her feel safe and special.

Instead, he closed her fingers over the kiss and released her hand. Her heart froze and it was hard to breathe. Heat continued to blow against her face and the radio played softly, so quiet she couldn't make out the words.

"Penelope, you know that your dad is looking for a husband for you, and we need to talk about that."

Never those words. She had never expected that from him. She shivered in the warmth of the truck cab and crossed her arms in front of herself. Slowly she nodded, because she couldn't answer.

Humiliation seeped through her, heating her face, making her want to run, to not look at him. She wondered if her father knew how it felt to be her. Who in the world wanted to be known as the heiress who couldn't find someone to love her? The heiress who needed her father to find her a suitable match?

"Penelope, I was one of the men."

Not that. He could tell her that he was leaving and that he'd probably never see her again...*anything but that.* Her heart cracked a little and all warmth seeped out of her, leaving her fingers frozen and trembling. Tears stung her eyes and she blinked to keep them from falling.

"So this isn't friendship, this is courting, Herman Lear style?" She meant to add acid to her tone, instead she sounded young and pathetic.

"No." The one word was loud in the silent cab of the truck. "No, this isn't about your dad. That's why I'm telling you this. I think we're friends and I wanted you to know the truth, in case your dad said something or tried to imply something else."

"Right." She reached for the truck handle. "I think I'll go now."

"Don't. I'll drive you to the B and B."

"I'd rather you didn't. I'd like to go sulk by myself, alone, with no one to see my humiliation."

"You shouldn't be humiliated."

She laughed at that. "Of course not. At least he was careful in picking men a lot like himself. After all, a Lear needs a strong, wealthy man who knows how to handle his career and his women."

"That isn't fair. I did say no."

"That makes it much better, the fact that you rejected me before you ever met me. Now I'm just swimming in self-confidence."

"Don't..."

"No, don't say anything. You have no idea how humiliating this is."

He reached for her hand.

She shook her head. Tears were streaming down her cheeks, hot against cool flesh. She jumped out of the truck, slamming the door behind her and wishing she could have slammed it hard enough for everyone to hear her frustration and anger. Hard enough for her father to hear.

Frozen, she worked the top buttons of her coat with trembling fingers as tears blurred her vision and she fought to blink them away. The truck she'd escaped from followed her, the headlights beating a path on the ice as tires crunched in the snow. She glanced back but kept walking.

She didn't need him to follow her, to get her back to safety. A short time ago he'd been her friend. Now he was just another person her father had put in her life. And he'd rejected her.

How could she ever look him in the eyes again, knowing that?

The cracking of her heart felt like a fault line about to give way to a major quake. She shook from the inside out, partially from cold, partially from rage and mostly from the pain.

She wanted someone to like her—no, to love her for herself.

The truck stopped behind her as she hurried up the steps and into the B and B. The clerk behind the desk smiled. He was new. She didn't like him either. He always smiled like he knew something about her.

For that matter, she really thought she'd seen him next to the door to her room. He's said he wanted to check and see if she needed more towels.

She glared at him as she rushed up the stairs to the third floor. So much for finding peace this year at Christmas. And what about being thankful at Thanksgiving? Maybe this was a sign that it was time to go home. Or maybe it was time to go anywhere but here?

Tucker didn't get much sleep, which was the reason for drinking three cups of coffee the next morning before he went to a meeting with Amy's tour guides. There wasn't much going on in the way of tours, not in November, but there were still a few people hunting for treasure.

It was crazy, but no one wanted his opinion. People had gotten injured. Amy's house had been broken into. Penelope had gotten lost. It made no sense.

As Tucker sat there listening, he wondered what people thought they'd find, if and when they found this treasure. He knew what they wanted to find. He knew why the town was crazy to find the treasure. But who found hidden, buried treasures? In the real world, pretty much nobody.

But enough people were interested to keep this little town going, and to keep Reed Truscott busy with potential crooks. Tucker had talked to Reed about the guy lurking near the B and B and Reed had suggested he show up for this meeting, to see if any of the guys working as tour guides looked familiar.

Reed had showed up, too. Not that he was looking for potential thugs. He seemed more interested in Amy. Tucker smiled, and smiling hadn't been too easy since last night, when Penelope jumped out of his truck.

Not that he blamed her for being angry. Now that he thought about it, he realized what her father had done to her. That would make a woman feel pretty low in the pecking order, to have her father arranging her life that way. And to realize the Lear fortune wasn't enough to drag someone in.

Or at least not someone that could match her.

Anger seethed inside him, taking him by surprise. He was mad at her father and mad at every man that had turned her down and hurt her, including himself.

But she wasn't his problem.

He was the same guy that had let his dad down. He was the guy who had set a drunk loose to kill an innocent girl. He was the guy just starting to find a way back from all of his own guilt, and he didn't really have time to be saddled with the guilt of what Herman Lear had done to his daughter.

That wasn't his reason for being at this meeting, though. They were looking for two things: crooks and stalkers. So much for quiet small-town life. As he scanned the group, not one of the tour guides looked like the man he'd seen near the inn. He glanced Reed's way and shook his head. "Not here."

"We'll keep looking."

Amy was talking about fishing, hunting and a few other things that Tucker didn't need a guide for and didn't intend on guiding someone else to do. He stood up and whispered that he'd catch Reed later.

On his way out the door, he decided to walk around the inn and see if he could spot anything that the man he'd seen had left behind. He passed a little business that specialized in planning weddings, Bethany Marlow's shop. He remembered hearing that she'd recently come back to town to plan weddings and she'd gotten herself engaged to Nate McMann. Tucker itched a little at all of these engagements.

He glanced inside and watched the spectacle, with no idea why it meant so much to a woman to put on all of that lace. Delilah stood in front of Bethany, a book in her hand. Planning a wedding that wasn't even proposed, or so he'd heard at the coffee shop. Another woman stood in front of the mirror, a gauzy veil over her face. She wore jeans and a big sweater. When she turned, he realized it was Penelope. Pink crawled into her cheeks and she turned away.

Someone would marry her. He thought her dad had found a perfect match: the guy with the right business connections. In the end, that's what it was all about for Herman Lear.

He walked on down the street, trying hard to push Penelope from his mind, but not managing to. He remembered the two of them singing about building a snowman named Parson Brown. He pictured her in that veil, standing in front of a snowman in a top hat.

She wouldn't appreciate that image.

He pictured her as the kind of woman who wanted a big wedding in a big cathedral. She'd want all the bells and whistles.

She was Alaska society to the hilt. He was a cheese sandwich kind of guy who had done well for himself. When he got married, he wanted a woman who would be as happy with a cheese sandwich as she was with lobster.

He'd been telling himself that for a long time. He hadn't put a priority on marrying, but when he did he'd find a woman who'd be everything his mother wasn't. She wouldn't be the type of woman who always wanted more and was never happy with what she had.

The wife he picked would be thrilled with a walk in the woods and elated with quiet nights at home. She wouldn't want the country club or a beach house.

His mother had been after those things. She'd gotten them, too. With three different husbands.

Forever wasn't in her dictionary.

But a woman who tried on a wispy veil and sang about Parson Brown? She might be different. She'd had it all, and now she wanted life without everything. Or so she thought.

But for how long? How long until she got bored with charming small-town life? What if she married Joe the logger and lived in a nice little house, had a few kids? And then left someday while the kids were at school?

Today he was going to tell Gordon Baker that he'd changed his mind. He was done with all of this marriage nonsense and treasure hunting. He was heading back to Seattle.

Chapter Fourteen

The diner was crowded. Penelope moved over to let Joleen sit next to her in the booth. Delilah sat across from them. All three of them were living different lives than they'd planned for themselves in Treasure Creek. Last night, Joleen had slowed down, calmed herself and had a real conversation with Harry.

Delilah was planning a wedding because she was thirty, and she said a woman ought to be married by then. Joleen shrugged that off because she had been happy and single for quite some time.

Penelope answered Delilah's question about the map. Of course she'd seen it.

"Do you think you know where the treasure is?" Delilah stirred sugar into her hot tea. "Someone thought you had a good idea."

"I have an idea."

"Then why aren't you out finding it?" Joleen glanced toward the door, as if her radar had picked up Harry Peters's entrance.

The shop owner turned a little red and headed in the opposite direction. Joleen frowned and tears filled her eyes. "I'm an idiot with men. I just scare the tar out of them."

"Relax." Delilah rolled expressive lined eyes. "Now tell me, Penelope, what about the treasure."

"I think I know. I'm just not sure, and I don't want to create a crazy stampede. I've talked to Amy about what I think."

"Oh, this is exciting." Joleen tried to reenter the conversation. Her gaze was still on Harry.

"It's exciting." Penelope glanced at her watch. "I have an appointment with Amy about food for the Thanksgiving dinner next week."

"Oh, my goodness, Thanksgiving already." Delilah chewed on her bottom lip. "Why can't I feel Thankful."

Joleen snorted, "'Cause, honey, you're afraid you're one holiday closer to being an old maid."

Delilah didn't laugh. Penelope patted her hand. "I have to go, but you two have a good time. I'll see you this evening at church."

"See you then, honey." Joleen scooted to let her out.

Penelope left the two to argue out their problems, and she hurried out the door and around the corner. She was meeting Amy at the inn.

As she rounded the corner she hit a solid wall of chest, and the odor of onions and garlic. She backed up, ready to apologize. Instead she tried to scream. A hand clasped over her mouth and cold steel hit her neck.

She tried to think about self-defense, about where to hit, how to kick. He had her arms behind her and she couldn't get her legs to cooperate.

"Keep your mouth shut, sweetie, and you might not get hurt."

She nodded, but her mind was racing, thinking over the safety tips she'd learned over the years. Never go willingly. Always leave something. Turn on your cell phone. She tried to get her hand into her pocket, but he saw the direction she was going and reached first, grabbing her cell phone and tossing it.

"Not a good idea." A second man laughed at her. She glanced around. No one in sight. She couldn't run, they had her tight against them.

She had to do something.

The pearl necklace around her neck. Her grandmother's necklace. She reached for it, grabbing it before they could stop her. She pulled, and pearls went clattering along the sidewalk.

"Oh, aren't you a smart one." One of her captors squeezed her hand. "Don't pull another stunt like that or you won't survive this."

Okay, so what did they want?

They dragged her down the sidewalk, away from town, away from help. The one with the gun leaned in close.

"I'm going to take my hand off your mouth, but you keep your trap shut and just do what I say or I'll have to shoot you."

She nodded. His hand moved slowly. She weighed her odds. Scream and he might shoot. Or they might hide her. She didn't see a soul around who could help. She shivered and pulled her crocheted scarf around her neck. Loose pieces of yarn. She'd meant to fix it. With her free hand she tugged a few from the yarn fringe and let them flutter to the ground.

"What do you want from me?"

A ransom. She was sure of it. What other value did she have?

"The treasure. I heard you talking about your secret memory, and the map you've got in your head. Well, we've got the real map but we need for you to tell us what you know. I want you to lead us to that treasure." The big oaf who smelled like onions and cigarettes leaned closer and she nearly gagged.

"I don't know where it is. If I knew, I'd have told Amy."

"I think you have an idea."

She nodded. "I do have an idea."

She pretended to fiddle with her scarf. A few more fringes came loose. She really hoped someone would notice.

"Then you'd better share your idea."

She tripped over the sidewalk, and as she righted herself she dropped a card from Bethany's business. Her brilliant abductors were clueless.

"Down the trail. I think they used to call it the Creek Trail. But not now. I can't remember what they call it, but if you follow it far enough it lead to the Chilkoot."

"You have a photographic memory. Of course you remember."

"I haven't seen it. I know what I saw on the map. I saw a rock formation on that trail. There's an old settler's cabin near the rocks."

"That's where we're going. You'd better have your walking shoes on."

She looked down at the shoes she wore every day. There really weren't any other kind suitable for Treasure Creek and the amount of walking she did each day. Shoes. Her mother would be proud that at a moment like this her mind turned to shoes. She wanted to cry because that wasn't who she was.

It wasn't who she wanted to be. And this was the time in her life when she'd really have to prove that there was more to Penelope Lear than a bank account and good fashion sense.

If she wanted to survive, she was going to have to be strong and outsmart the two men who had taken her captive. She grimaced and shuddered a little. Outsmarting them wouldn't be a stretch. Getting away from them might prove to be difficult.

The cabin she'd told them about was several miles from town. That meant a long, long walk on a cold day.

Tucker tried to ignore Jake and Reed. The two men waved, called his name and then hurried across the street to stop him from getting in his truck. He wasn't leaving yet, just thinking about loading his truck. Obviously, they thought it was up to them to stop him.

"Have you seen Penelope Lear?" Reed put a hand on Tucker's truck door.

Tucker was a little offended by that. He thought about moving Reed's hand, but he really didn't want to push the cop's buttons. "I haven't seen Penelope. Why?

"She's missing. She's been gone since yesterday. And today we found her cell phone by the diner."

That changed everything. Tucker should have checked on her. He should have made sure he got back to her place safely. She wasn't his responsibility. He walked away from the two men that he considered friends.

He'd done a lot of making excuses. His dad had pushed him away, and it had been easier to allow it than to fight it. Tucker should have pushed back. He'd taken good money for defense in that DWI case.

Guilty. Tucker was guilty on every charge. Penelope had needed his protection, even if he hadn't wanted to do it and she hadn't realized she needed it.

But he was done with this town and guilt. He walked back to his truck and Jake put a hand on his shoulder. "Do you know where she might be?"

"Have you contacted her parents? Maybe she went back to Anchorage?"

"They're on their way here. She hasn't talked to them for three days, not since the day she called and disowned them for trying to buy her a husband."

"Right." He kept a hand on the truck door and tried to think fast. Had she left, had something happened?

"Do you know where she might be?" Jake pushed.

"Not a clue, but I plan on finding her." That settled inside him, and he tried to make sense of it.

This was about not wanting to feel guilty again. He let that thought roll through his mind, and it didn't make him feel any better. This was about wanting to find her, because he wanted her safe. He wanted her in his arms.

He needed her in his arms and close.

"Have you talked to anyone?"

Reed pulled out a notepad. "Yeah, we've talked to people. We talked to Delilah and Joleen. They had lunch with her yesterday. We talked to the night clerk where she was staying, and to a guy that Amy hired. He'd asked some questions about Penelope that Amy didn't like."

"Do you think he has something to do with it?"

Reed shook his head. "He clammed up. But I don't know if it is about this or something else."

"Okay, let's go." Tucker opened his truck door.

"Not that quick. We need more to go on than a dumped cell phone. You seem to know her better than anyone," Reed said as he stuck the paper back in his pocket. "Maybe you can think of something, or see something, that we missed."

He knew her as well as anyone. He brushed a hand through his hair and nodded.

"Where'd you find her cell?"

"Side street just down from the diner," Jake offered.

"Let's go there. Maybe you missed something?"

They drove down the street to the area where Penelope's cell phone was found. Tucker parked and got out of his truck. Reality was colder than November in Alaska. It encased his heart, making him hurt like crazy and then making him numb.

The reality of it was that he didn't want to lose Penelope Lear.

Where was she?

He walked, thinking about her, about who

would take her. The sidewalk was uneven and icy in spots. He scanned the area, thinking about the last time he'd seen her and how hurt she'd been. Those thoughts wouldn't help find her.

He looked at the curb and then leaned for a better look before he reached down to grab something familiar. "What about these?" He showed them a few pearls.

Reed shook his head. "They could belong to anyone."

"No, they're hers." Tucker didn't have to think about it, he knew. "She wore them everywhere. I never saw her without those pearls. I think they were her grandmother's. That's what she told Wilma Johnson."

He bent and started picking them up. She'd want those pearls. He shoved them in his pockets. Jake bent and picked up a few.

"Tucker, we don't have time for this." Reed handed him a few pearls.

"You had wait until today before you told me she was missing."

"I know you love her, but…" Jake backed down and shut up when Tucker looked up at him. "I mean, Reed didn't know she was missing until Amy said she didn't show up for practice this morning."

"Someone should have noticed." Tucker stood back up, his hand full of pearls that he shoved into his pocket. "And she's a friend."

"Right, a friend."

Tucker walked past Jake and kept going. A block away he noticed something that he'd ignored until that moment. Yarn. He'd seen it on the sidewalk and now at the head of the trail that led out of town, along the creek and down to a few old historic home sites.

"They took her down this trail." He looked back, waiting for Reed and Jake to catch up.

"Why do you say that?" Reed looked around. "There are a dozen or more places that she could have walked to from here."

Tucker held up the yarn and a button. "Her scarf and her button."

He knew her that well. It took him by surprise.

"Okay, let me radio back to the station and call Amy." Reed stepped away from them. He came back a few minutes later. "Amy is driving down here. She's bringing supplies, and she said we aren't going down this trail without her. She said if we find Penelope, she'll need another woman."

That filled Tucker's mind with thoughts that caused him to clench his fists and think pretty dark thoughts on what he'd do to the person that took Penelope. If these people had hurt her...

"Tucker, we'll find her." Jake stood at his side.

"Yeah, we'll find her." Tucker wanted to take off, to let Jake and Reed catch up. He stayed, though.

The best way to help Penelope was to keep his head on straight. Penelope had obviously done the same. He smiled, kind of proud of her for leaving a trail they could follow. And he had no doubt that she'd meant all of this to be a way for help to find her.

She didn't need any of them, but, man, he needed her. He raked a hand through his hair and let out a sigh when Amy's car stopped at the side of the road. She jumped out with a backpack and walkie-talkies. That's what made Penelope and Amy friends. The two had been raised in different worlds, but they were a lot alike.

"Let's go find her." Reed started down the trail and Tucker walked next to him.

"No one has asked for money—a ransom?"

"Nothing." Reed shifted his gaze from one side of the trail to the other. Tucker did the same, looking for more clues. He saw a business card and bent to pick it up. It was from Bethany's. The wedding planner. He handed the card to Reed, who took it and shoved it in his pocket.

"Someone was after her, but why?" Jake echoed what they were all thinking.

Tucker thought about it. He'd thought about it a lot, since back at the cabin when he'd first found her and first found footprints outside. Who would want her and why? He hadn't been able to imagine why anyone would want a chattering female who had a penchant for getting into trouble.

Now he knew more about her. He knew reasons why he would want her in his life. He would want her because she made him smile. She was an optimist. She had faith. She knew how to think ahead, and think quick.

But who had taken her and why? He knew why he wanted her, but why would someone kidnap her?

Without a ransom demand, he doubted it was about her dad's fortune. That led Tucker to one conclusion: the treasure. She *knew* that map. Without having it in her hand, she had it in her mind. And people knew that. The same people who hadn't been able to get their hands on an original, or the people who had. Maybe they'd heard that she'd gone looking for the treasure because she thought she might know where it was located.

Those were the types of people who might want Penelope Lear. He should have thought about it sooner.

He told Reed and Jake what he thought. Reed agreed. Jake slapped him on the back.

"Tucker, stop beating yourself up for everything."

Yeah, Jake knew him that well.

She'd been tied up in the little cabin for more than twenty-four hours. Penelope had prayed and prayed that someone would find her trail. Every time she closed her eyes she pictured Tucker—his face, his smile.

Common sense always returned, and she remembered that he was just another man her father had brought into her life. But Tucker had been rejected, obviously. Her dad had settled on a man who had a similar background and whose family business would match well with their own.

Tucker had rejected her. She kept going back to that thought. Her dad had approached Tucker, and he hadn't wanted anything to do with her, with marriage to her.

Enough of that. She wasn't going to feel

sorry for herself. She was going to figure out a way to get out of this mess. She closed her eyes again and tried to think about a warm fireplace. Thinking about being warm was better than thinking about Tucker. She could hear the digging outside, shovels hitting dirt and stone.

They hadn't caught on yet that she'd given them the wrong location. They were digging away, but she knew that the real spot was somewhere else on this property. She was sure of it. She was nearly positive the treasure was buried near a tree, or a stump.

They were digging near the stream. She smiled. Knowing she had fooled them did give her a little comfort. The fire they'd built, which really wasn't much of a fire, provided no comfort at all.

Her stomach growled painfully. They'd shoved some bread in her mouth that morning. It had been stale, dry and tasteless. She imagined pecan waffles at Lizbet's. And coffee. She could really use a cup of coffee.

Tucker. She closed her eyes and tried to push away his image, his smile. Instead of dwelling on what she couldn't have, she dwelt on prayer. It had become pretty obvious that if she was going to get out of here, God was going to have to do the rescuing.

"Please, God, send help. What more is there to say? I mean, I could go on and on, but the only thing I really need is help."

She wondered if He heard. He obviously had other, pretty important issues to deal with. Around the world people were hurting and in trouble. Did she rate high enough for God to put all of His other duties on hold to help her?

The thoughts seemed pretty close to delirious. If they didn't find her soon, she'd be a goner.

The door opened. The man who carried the gun entered. She forced a bright smile because his face was red, either from anger or exertion. He tossed the pan of something they'd cooked for themselves. Oh, anger. She bit down on her bottom lip and went for the scared female routine.

"Where's the treasure?" He slammed his hand down on the old table a short distance away.

"I don't know. If I knew where it was, I'd have dug it up. I told you what was on the map. That's as good as I can do."

"You need to do better." He picked up a pen and tossed it on the table and then he pulled a knife out of a drawer.

This was it, then. She'd die here, today. He walked toward her with the knife and she prayed hard. She closed her eyes and when she did, he slit the ropes on her hands and pushed her out of the chair.

"Draw the map."

"Oh, okay." She glanced around, looking for something to draw on. That's when she saw movement outside the cabin. Her heart picked up speed and pounded so hard it hurt to breathe.

"Draw it." Tom—that's what the other man had called him—pointed to the piece of paper he'd put down in front of her.

"Okay, I will." Her hands were free. Her feet weren't tied.

She considered the odds. She could make a run for it and pray that it was Tucker outside, or she could wait and hope for the best.

With hands that trembled, she started the drawing. Tom relaxed and sat down.

"Will you share the treasure with me?" Penelope really couldn't believe he was so stupid he didn't know who she was.

Tom grunted. "Doubt it. Might be able to persuade me to keep you around, though. I'd probably buy you some pearls to replace the ones you lost."

Her grandmother's pearls. She couldn't talk, because if she said anything about those pearls she'd cry. She also couldn't glance out the window, because that would surely lead Tom to look out also. She didn't want to give away any rescuer who might be attempting to locate her.

"This is it." Tucker leaned against a tree a short distance from the cabin. Amy took a quiet step forward and gasped.

"What?" Reed stood behind her, his hand moving toward her waist, and then back to his side. Tucker smiled at Jake, because they'd both noticed.

"This is it, Reed. This is the spot on the map. They brought Penelope here. Or maybe she brought them."

Tucker groaned. "Her photographic memory. They made her lead them to the treasure."

And this was about as ridiculous and far-fetched as a late-night movie. People didn't get kidnapped or find treasure this way. But then, maybe sometimes they did.

Tucker moved a few steps forward, searching for Penelope. She was in there somewhere. He hoped she was in there. He prayed, really prayed that she was alive. His gaze landed on the man by the stream, digging in an area that was more rocks than dirt.

Penelope had told them to dig there, but Amy was pointing to a tree. She was practically bouncing in a silent pantomime. After all of this, to find the treasure this way seemed pretty unbelievable. It didn't matter to Tucker. What mattered to him was that Penelope was inside that cabin and he didn't know if she was injured, or if she was even alive.

Until she let out a banshee scream that pierced the quiet afternoon. The four of them, Tucker, Jake, Reed and Amy, rushed into the clearing. As they headed toward the cabin, Jake headed for the thug by the river. Divide and conquer.

Penelope ran out of the cabin. She was almost to the steps when a man hurled himself at her. She turned, did a great roundhouse kick and then punched him in the face. She really *did* know karate. The thug staggered back and she ran down the steps toward them. Jake had the other guy by the arms and was dragging him forward.

Tucker pulled Penelope close, holding her against him. She breathed hard and tears wetted his neck. He didn't have time to think or react. Suddenly the man from the porch was coming at them with a gun pointed at Amy, who had gotten a short distance away from the rest of them, including Reed. She jumped back, but he caught her hard against him, pulling her away from Tucker. Reed had gone to help Jake.

"No," Penelope cried. "Let her go. I helped you find this place. We don't want the treasure. Just let Amy go."

"No, I don't think so. You all stand back and I'll let her go. But I want you men on the ground, arms outstretched." The thug held Amy close, the gun to her head.

Tucker shot Reed a look. Reed shook his head and went down. They were going to let these guys go. Tucker knew it was the right thing to do. He knew it, but, man, he was itching to take them in, to make them pay for what they'd done. As he went down, he kept his eyes on Amy, on the guy with the gun.

"Stay on the ground for five minutes." The guy shouted, still holding a gun on Amy. "Do you understand?"

"We understand." Reed's voice shook with emotion. Tucker drew in a deep breath and fought the urge to ignore the warning and go after the men.

He looked up as the men were moving

away, Amy still at gunpoint. They were to the clearing when they pushed her aside and ran.

Reed and Jake were on their feet and chasing after the two while Tucker helped Amy to her feet.

"Let them go," Amy brushed her hands down the sides of her jeans. But she was already moving in the direction of Penelope. "Are you okay? Did they hurt you?"

"I'm fine. I just couldn't find a way to get away from them."

"But you led them to the treasure." Amy hugged her tight. "This is it, Penelope. We have our treasure."

Tucker watched the edge of the woods and breathed a sigh of relief when Jake and Reed returned. They didn't have the two thugs with them. "Where are they?"

"Got away." Reed hurried toward Amy, but he didn't reach for her. Tucker thought he ought to go ahead and just hug her. Instead the two smiled at one another. "You okay?"

She nodded, smiling big. "Better than okay. They led us to the treasure. Or should I say, Penelope led them to the treasure. And then she told them it was by the creek."

"It isn't?" Reed looked around. "So?"

"If I'm not mistaken, this is the cabin I've read about in old history journals. And that tree is where the treasure is buried."

Tucker grabbed a shovel and handed it to her. It was her treasure, she should get to dig. They all took turns, but in the end, Amy's shovel hit the box. Tucker stepped back and watched as she pulled it free. He glanced in Penelope's direction and she was smiling with tears streaming down her cheeks. This was what she'd wanted for Treasure Creek. She'd wanted to give them this treasure.

"Open it." Reed stepped forward with a knife. "Maybe you can pry the lid."

Amy pulled the treasure box back from his grasp. "No."

Reed's brows scrunched together. "No?"

Amy shook her head. "We'll save it for the Christmas pageant. This box holds something that will change all our lives. I don't know exactly how, but I know that it will, and I want it to be special for all of us, for all of Treasure Creek."

"You can't be serious." Reed let out a loud sigh and Tucker could have told him that was a mistake.

"Yes, Reed, I'm serious. I make my own decisions and this is what I'm going to do."

"I think it's a great idea." Penelope hugged Amy tight. "I think it's perfect."

"What if it isn't anything valuable?" Jake scratched his cheek. "Seriously, Amy, what if it's just a time capsule?"

"I'm not listening to anyone. We're saving it for Christmas."

"Okay, we'll lock it up until then. We need to keep it safe. And keep you safe." Reed's gaze remained on Amy, and she nodded.

Tucker watched Penelope. She was steady on her feet and smiling, but her face was pale, and dark rings shadowed her eyes. They still didn't know what she'd been through or if she was hurt. Reed glanced her way.

"Penelope, are you going to be able to make this hike back to town?"

She nodded. "I can make it. I'm tired and hungry, but I'm ready to go home."

"Did they hurt you?" Reed continued his questioning and Tucker wanted to stop him. But Penelope shook her head.

"No."

They started down the trail, and as much as Tucker wanted to be the one at her side, Penelope walked next to Amy. The three men followed. It was getting dark and they would have to finish this journey in the black Alaskan evening. Tucker would have given a whole lot of treasure to be back in civilization right about then. He would have given a lot to have people around him who made rational decisions.

But Penelope was safe. She didn't seem to have a lot to say to him, but she was safe.

Chapter Fifteen

Penelope wasn't upset that her parents arrived in Treasure Creek the evening after she was rescued. It felt good to be with them. Her brother had accompanied them and she didn't mind being teased about spa days and manicures. She could even admit that she wouldn't mind a good manicure. And after everything was over she managed to talk her family into staying in Treasure Creek for Thanksgiving dinner at the end of the week.

"How long are you staying?" Penelope walked next to her brother as they left the police station. She glanced back over her shoulder, wanting a last glimpse of Tucker. He was gone. She wondered if he was going to finish loading his truck and head back to Seattle before Thanksgiving.

"I'm staying to eat with you all tomorrow, and then I have business in Hawaii."

"Business?"

"Maybe not so much business." David walked with quick, long strides, his overcoat flapping. The cold never seemed to bother him.

"I guess I'm going home." She tossed a quick look back at her parents. "I need to settle down and stop putting myself in danger."

"It wouldn't hurt." David winked, and his smile softened his angular face. "Pen, do what you want to do. Don't marry some guy that you don't like just because he has the right pedigree or his parents own the right piece of property. Do what you want. If you want to feed children or run a shelter, do it. If you want to get married and stay in Treasure Creek, then stick to your guns and tell Dad that you've made a decision."

"Right. That's easy for *you* to say."

"Not really, I had to fight to build the business I wanted."

"Maybe it's just easier to go home."

He laughed then. "As if you've ever done the easy thing."

"I'm not that bad."

"No, you're not bad, you're just strong-willed. Tell me, sis, what is it that you love about this town? I'm just not seeing it. No night life, not much in the way of restaurants."

She thought it should be obvious. "It's the people, David. They have so much faith and so much love for each other."

"Got it." He glanced around and she wondered if he saw what she saw when she looked at Treasure Creek, or did he just see another small town?

"I see a town that needs a real resort." He nodded as he made the observation.

"No, David, not here. Please don't do that to Treasure Creek. It would ruin everything."

"Seriously? You don't want a resort here, with a spa and a classy boutique?"

"No, I don't."

"I doubted you, Pen, but I think you really have changed."

Ahead of them, she saw Tucker Lawson walk out of Gordon Baker's law office. He didn't look her way. She wondered if that was on purpose. Not that it should matter.

"Isn't that *the* Tucker Lawson, your hero?" David nudged her a little and she slid on the ice. He grabbed her arm. "Sorry, I didn't know you could be knocked off your feet."

"Very funny. He isn't my hero."

"Of course not." David stopped to look for cars before they crossed over to Lizbet's for lunch. "Hey, so what about this treasure? Did you peek in the box?"

"No. Amy insisted it be opened in December, as a Christmas gift to the town."

David shook his head. "What if it's just a rusty old box with a few crumbled newspaper clippings?"

"Then I guess everyone will be disappointed."

Including Penelope.

But she had already been disappointed. Tucker was leaving. He hadn't even said goodbye.

Tucker stood next to Jake, both wearing tuxedos. The big difference was that Jake was smiling as if he had discovered something more valuable than a long-lost treasure. Bethany, wedding planner extraordinaire, or so Casey had informed them, was fiddling with the collar and telling Jake to stop slouching.

"Seriously, Jake, couldn't we do something less formal, something with jeans and boots, maybe corduroy?" Tucker pulled at the neck of his shirt.

"No, we're not doing something less formal. This is what Casey wants."

Bethany took a straight pin out of her mouth and shot Tucker a look that he assumed was supposed to put him in his place. "A wedding is important for a woman. It's our big event. We want it to be perfect."

"I thought the marriage should be the real event. The wedding is the icing. If the cake is stale, the icing doesn't matter." Tucker grumbled, and he didn't mind that he was testy.

"You've obviously never been in love," Bethany chided, heading his way with straight pins. He didn't cringe, but he had the good sense to hope she wasn't going to stick him.

"I guess I haven't been." Tucker stood still as she pinned and lectured him about his posture. He thought about telling her he wasn't a schoolgirl going to the prom. He didn't care about posture or the length of his jacket hem.

But she was talking about love and forever, and for some crazy reason her rambling made him think about Penelope. He hadn't seen her since the day they rescued her. They'd brought her back to town and to her waiting parents, and the Lears had circled the wagons, keeping her surrounded by family and "people."

The people worked for her father, Tucker assumed. He also assumed they were packing. Herman Lear wasn't taking any chances with his little girl.

But she wasn't a little girl. Tucker glanced

out the window and ignored Bethany's constant chatter about weddings being special and how lucky Casey was to have such a beautiful wedding. And wouldn't it be lovely to have Jake's daughter as the bridesmaid.

Tucker grunted because he wasn't commenting on that little chick. He knew when to leave well enough alone and this was one of those times. Veronica was ornery, pure and simple.

As he glanced around the little shop, his eye caught and held on something he'd seen before.

"That veil over there." He pointed and Bethany slapped his arm down.

"What about it."

"Is it reserved, or whatever it is you do with things like that?" Heat crawled up his cheeks and he avoided looking at Jake.

Bethany stood and turned to look at the veil. "Oh, no, it isn't. Someone ordered it, and then she changed her mind."

"About the veil?"

Bethany laughed, "No, she changed her mind about the groom."

"Oh." Tucker wanted that veil. His mouth went dry thinking about Penelope standing in this shop in front of the mirror, that gauzy piece of nothing covering her face.

"Tuck, you okay?" Jake cleared his throat. "You aren't going to pass out are you?"

"Women pass out."

Bethany pinned his jacket. "No, men pass out. They forget to loosen their knees while they're standing here. Pretty soon, down they go."

"I'm not going to pass out." His heart hammered and his brain felt foggy, but he was pretty sure it was about an epiphany, and about an image of Penelope Lear standing at the altar with that veil covering her face, and not about his knees being locked.

"You're pretty pale." Bethany stepped back. "I'm done with you."

Tucker stepped down off the stool she had him standing on for thirty minutes, and walked over to pick up the veil. It was soft, not crisp the way he had thought a veil might be. "I want this."

"It won't suit you." Jake walked over to the counter to pay Bethany. "But I'll buy the veil if he really wants it."

"I'm buying the veil."

Bethany stood behind the counter. "Whatever for?"

Tucker shrugged. "For kicks."

Or because he wanted to see it on Penelope one more time. And he wanted her in a white dress when she wore it.

What town had a Thanksgiving meal that included nearly everyone in the community? The next evening, Tucker knew the answer to that question. Treasure Creek was such a town. They took community to an entirely new level. He stood inside the great hall that was lined with tables, and watched as people took seats. Someone handed him a pitcher of water.

Now, what did he do with that?

"Fill the glasses." Penelope stood next to him. Man, she smelled good. He wanted to lean in and pull her close, not fill glasses with water.

"Fine. I can do that." Fill glasses, that is. She had a tub of rolls, and as they walked, she filled baskets on the table.

"My parents are here."

"I know. I said hello." He had actually talked to her father earlier that day. It had been a busy day, getting ready for his drive back to Seattle, doing some work around the house, and talking to Herman Lear.

"They like you." Penelope glanced back over her shoulder. Her hair fell forward and she brushed it back. "I'm staying, you know."

"I thought you were going back to Anchorage."

"No, I told my dad that I'm staying here. I bought a house and I'm going to do some work with Dr. Havens."

"Really?"

"Yes, really."

"Could you promise me something?"

She stopped filling baskets. "What?"

He leaned forward—close. "Get a GPS and don't go into the woods alone."

"You're very funny." But she laughed, and he was glad.

They finished, and he followed her back to the table where her parents were sitting. "Mind if I join you all?"

Penelope looked surprised. He doubted if she noticed that no one else in her family looked too shocked. Instead, her brother moved down a seat, giving Tucker the place next to Penelope.

Crowds of people were moving through the building, finding seats, moving to new locations with old friends. Penelope sat very quietly next to Tucker. Finally, she turned to look at him.

"I thought you were leaving, going back to Seattle."

"I had unfinished business." He reached for the basket of bread and offered her a roll. She shook her head and he passed the basket to David.

"I see."

"Could we talk later?" Tucker whispered close to her ear, because this really didn't need to be the latest bit of news to run through the grapevine.

"I suppose."

"After we eat?"

"Of course."

What if this didn't go the way he'd planned? Tucker hadn't really let himself think that until now. He hadn't allowed himself to think that she might not feel what he felt. Even as the thought tried to surface, he pushed it back down. He was going to be an optimist if it killed him.

Penelope couldn't stop the trembling in her hands. All through the meal, rather than thinking of all that she was thankful for, she thought about Tucker sitting next to her and Tucker wanting to talk to her. He looked so serious.

She tried to avoid looking at him. Instead,

she watched Joleen talk to Harry. Joleen, kind of calm, her voice quiet, and Harry not looking completely cornered or stricken. Penelope was proud of herself for talking Joleen through the finer steps of courting. The gist of it had been about not coming on too strong.

And Delilah. They'd met together for a women's prayer meeting.

Her brother, David, had been wrong. There was plenty to do in Treasure Creek. There weren't any country clubs, and the restaurants weren't fancy, but life was good in this small community. And the new beauty parlor, where she'd gotten her hair done, was hiring a manicurist and a massage therapist.

The dinner she had looked forward to fell apart, though. She couldn't eat with Tucker sitting next to her, talking to the people around them as if everything was great.

Of course, maybe it was great for Tucker Lawson. He was settling up his life here and heading back to Seattle. He'd found the faith he'd lost as a child. He had reconnected with his friends. He'd forgiven himself. She could see in his face, in the way his hazel eyes flashed with warmth, that life was better for him.

"Stop looking so sad." He leaned close to her ear, and the way he brushed close to her cheek felt as if he had kissed her. He even paused close to her ear.

She closed her eyes. "I'm not sad. I am going to miss you."

There, she'd said it. And when she did, a tear sneaked out and slid down her cheek. He caught it with his finger and then he brushed his hand across her cheek as gently as if he were touching a hummingbird.

"Come with me." He scooted his chair back and she slid hers out, but then she hesitated.

If she left with him, she'd fall apart in his arms. She might actually beg him to take her father up on his offer. She might tell him that she'd never loved anyone the way she loved him. She might forget all of the good advice she'd given Joleen and come on too strong.

"Pen, go with the man." David winked and gave her a light push when she couldn't quite make her feet move.

It was suddenly a good idea to leave, because tears were burning her eyes and she thought she might be about to fall apart. Lost, abducted, nearly married off to the highest bidder, and now she was losing it? That was ridiculous. She was a Lear. She took a deep breath and pulled it together to follow Tucker outside.

He reached for her hand, and they walked

side by side down the street. Christmas lights twinkled around them and they could hear the music from the Christmas store.

"Where are we going?"

"To the park."

"It's cold to be out for a walk." She shivered inside the down coat and Tucker's arm went around her, pulling her close.

"Remember when you sang 'Winter Wonderland.'"

"And you didn't appreciate it."

He laughed and she leaned closer to him. He sang the lyrics about building a snowman.

She laughed and finished with naming him Parson Brown.

Tucker reached for her hand and pulled her in the direction of the park. "I have to show you what I made for you."

His voice was husky and light. He hurried and she nearly had to run. "Tucker, slow down."

"I can't." He laughed and led her on. "'He'll say are you married, we'll say no, man…'"

He stopped and Penelope stopped next to him, her breath freezing in her lungs. The park twinkled with snow and Christmas lights. In the middle of it all was a snowman. He wore a top hat and red scarf, and a Bible was on a little stand in front of him.

"Tucker?"

He pulled her close. "I found Parson Brown."

"I see." But she didn't, and tears were rolling down her cheeks, warm on her cold flesh. She tried to brush them away, but more fell.

Tucker leaned and kissed them away. His lips brushed hers and then settled, kissing her until it didn't matter that it was November in Alaska and snow was falling. Or maybe that's what made it all perfect. It was cold, but his arms around her were warm and he'd built her a snowman on Thanksgiving.

He held her close and his breath was soft near her ear. "I have something else for you."

When he pulled back his hand went to his pocket. He pulled out the gossamer veil she'd tried on at Bethany's. As she stood there trembling, from cold and from the moment, he slid the veil over her head.

"I saw you in this. I think when I did, I knew that I wanted to be the one to lift it from your face, to hear a minister pronounce us husband and wife."

He lifted the veil and carefully moved it back, and then he cupped her cheeks in his gloved hands. "Penelope Lear, I asked your father today if he would allow me the honor of marrying his daughter."

Her lips and chin trembled. She bit down on her bottom lip, trying to hold it all together.

"What did he say?"

"He said you're a grown woman, and it is up to you. But he'd be proud to call me son."

"Oh."

"Oh?"

"I mean yes." And then she wrapped her arms around him and he held her close. "Yes, I want to be your wife. Yes, please marry me."

He pulled free again. "I forgot something important."

"What's that?"

"The ring. This was my grandmother's. It isn't new and the diamond isn't the biggest. If you want to pick a ring, I understand, but if not, I'd love for you to wear this ring. My grandmother wore it for sixty years."

"I want to wear it for seventy." She pulled off her glove and he slid the diamond-and-pearl ring onto her finger.

"I love you, Penelope Lear. I love you for who you are."

"I love you, too."

"So you'll marry me?" He leaned in and

kissed her, making it hard to breathe, hard to answer.

"I will, but I think maybe we should find a real minister."

"I'd like that very much."

He hugged her tight, and when they kissed again. Snow was falling, and they could heard carols being sung. Penelope Lear had a groom of her own and life had never been sweeter.

* * * * *

Dear Reader,

Welcome to Treasure Creek, Alaska. It was a privilege to work on this story and to spend a little time acquainting myself with the great state of Alaska. As I researched the area and pored over pictures of the landscape and the small towns, I could see why our characters would want to take off from their "real lives" and experience the great outdoors, Alaska-style.

Penelope Lear is a great heroine. To the outside world she had everything, but she felt as if she had nothing. She wanted more, and what she found was faith. I think she's like so many of us, searching to be who God called us to be and finding it in the most unlikely place.

Brenda Minton

QUESTIONS FOR DISCUSSION

1. When Tucker Lawson's father died, Tucker made a series of choices. The first was to leave Treasure Creek and fly to a cabin where he could think through his problems. He didn't turn to God, but how did God use the situation Tucker found himself in?

2. Penelope showed up in Treasure Creek because of an article. Do you think she was looking for romance or something else?

3. Penelope found faith in Treasure Creek. How does she first show that it changed her life?

4. In hunting for the treasure, Penelope seems to go off without thinking ahead. She has everything, so why would this treasure mean so much to her?

5. Faced with his father's death and the loss of a young woman he didn't know, Tucker isn't really searching for God. What is he looking for and how does that tie in to his lost faith?

6. The Johnsons have been living in this cabin for six months. They lost their son and they needed to find peace. How is their approach to grief the same as Tucker's and yet different?

7. Tucker doesn't want to like Penelope. He wants to believe she's just another selfish socialite. How does she show him that she is different?

8. Faced with the long walk back to Treasure Creek and unknown enemies, Tucker pushes everyone to keep going, including Penelope. How does she handle the situation and how does that change their relationship?

9. Penelope is attracted to Tucker, but she's looking for something more in life. Why is she holding back? He's wealthy. He's attractive. Isn't that enough?

10. Back in Treasure Creek, Penelope has to stand her ground when she is reunited with her parents. Why is this important for her future?

11. Tucker believes he's ready to head back to Seattle, even though he still has loose

ends to tie up with his father's estate. What continues to hold him to Treasure Creek?

12. Penelope is willing to do just about anything to help the town of Treasure Creek. She wants to find the treasure for the community. She is helping with the Christmas pageant. Does this have something to do with her history of going on trips to impoverished areas?

13. Does Penelope really know what she is searching for in life? Does she finally find that completeness in Treasure Creek?

14. Tucker is one of the men on Penelope's father's short list as a potential husband. Why would this be a problem for Penelope?

15. When do you believe Tucker really returns to his faith?